Awry With Dandelions

The Ardulum Series:

Ardulum: First Don

Ardulum: Second Don

Ardulum: Third Don

Tales from Ardulum

Ardulum: The Battle for Pruitcu

Other books by J.S. Fields:

Queen

Foxfire in the Snow

Distant Gardens

Farther Reefs

Awry With Dandelions

J.S. Fields

Space Wizard Science Fantasy

Raleigh, NC

Space Wizard Science Fantasy
Raleigh, NC
www.spacewizardsciencefantasy.com

Publisher's Note: This is a work of fiction. Names, characters,
places, and incidents are a product of the author's imagination.
Locales and public names are sometimes used for atmospheric
purposes. Any resemblance to actual people, living or dead, or
to businesses, companies, events, institutions, or locales is
completely coincidental.

Cover art by MoorBooks
Editing by Heather Tracy
Book Layout © 2015 BookDesignTemplates.com

Awry With Dandelions/J.S. Fields.— 1st ed.
ISBN 978-1-7350768-5-0

Author's website: www.jsfieldsbooks.com

To my younger self:
It's okay to not be ready.

CONTENTS

Note: Orin uses xie/xir pronouns in this story. Xie/xir is a nonbinary neopronoun, meaning Orin identifies neither as female nor male.

You can think of these pronouns like this:
He/she/xie
His/her/xir

Chapter 1

Orin stared at the wispy phantom, the edges of her bleeding into the dark corners of the dream. Not a ghost—not really—but a woman who existed, in theory, on Orin's planet. On Orin's continent, even. Not that Orin had ever met her in the flesh. For twenty damn years they'd visited each other every night as ghostly apparitions, and sporadically during the day. Sometimes Orin to Mette, sometimes the other way around, but the duration was always the same. Thirty seconds. No more, no less. They had collected the start of a thousand conversations but had never managed anything of real substance. The first few seconds were always disorienting. Then came the nausea. Then came the attempt at talking. Then it was over.

"Orin? Did you hear me?" Mette asked. "I said I think I've finally figured out how to separate our minds. We could sleep, Orin. Really sleep. We could be whole people, not genetically unrelated, mentally conjoined twins—don't make that face—however you want to describe us. Are you listening to me?"

Orin was listening, as much as xie could in a dream. Already xir feet wobbled on the increasingly unstable surface of xir bedroom floor—a memory's rendition and nothing more. Xie was still in bed. The room around Orin tilted. The sounds of morning, of the market, clinked along the false edges of their make-believe room. Even Mette canted, like her form had inserted into Orin's mind at a thirteen-degree tilt.

"I don't feel well," Orin said. Neither of them ever felt well. Not in the dreamscape, not when they were awake. Theirs was a chronic wasting sickness with no clear scientific, medical cause. Science came from Earth, with the colonists. But scientific principles from one planet didn't necessarily translate to another. Physics was guided by assumptions about reality, and reality didn't mean the same thing, planet to planet. Like how on Earth, you could make water from two hydrogens and an oxygen, and on Orin's planet you could also make it from saying seventeen nonsense words in the right order. On Earth horses lived just fine, and on this planet, Orin and Mette's planet, horses just died right out of the spaceship because no one had yet sorted how Orin's planet—and its magic—actually worked.

What did live well on Orin's planet? Komodo dragons. Obviously.

The phantom woman pulled at the corners of her embroidered nightgown. Orin saw little lutes on the fabric, or maybe lamps. The details were always best closest to Mette's face, where Orin could make out each solitary freckle on white skin, her dark brown eyes, and light brown hair. Orin's eyes were the same color but xir hair was far shorter and darker, xir skin tawny. Orin also refused to wear nightgowns. Nude was the only way to sleep, especially when you tended to wake up nauseous.

"You don't have to ignore me." Mette stomped to the edge of Orin's bed, nightdress dripping shades of rose in the moonlight.

Xie swallowed bile and tried to think of something to say. The sharp edges of Mette's cheekbones and jaw blurred. The dream slipped, fractionally at first, then in exponential segments, into drips of color. Not completely dissolving, but slipping away in desperate inches.

Orin's stomach knotted, and not from the intensity of their mental connection. This sounded too much like a real conversation—something they'd decided years ago was a lost cause. Thinking each other anything more than dreams caused too many problems. Orin had a good life. A semi-stable income. Xie'd learned to live with the inconvenience that was Mette, and fractured sleep, and persistently upset digestion. They'd tried to separate when they were younger—a mixture of near-death situations, magical potions that were probably just horrible herbal blends because Orin sure couldn't afford real magic, fright, and distance. Nothing had worked then, and nothing would work now. Orin wasn't willing, anymore, to court drowning or flinging xirself off a hillside to bounce Mette from xir brain, and xie couldn't imagine Mette wanted to keep pouring her family's seemingly endless money into herbalists and county fair witches. Not that they'd ever discussed money. But women in embroidered nightgowns generally had more cash than Orin saw in a year, and Mette had tried a new potion a week for almost six months before Orin had begged her to stop. The woman had the audacity of Methalimus royalty.

"No more, Mette. Can't we just give up? We're so tired, the both of us."

Mette put her hands on her hips and cocked her head, a pose she'd had since childhood. "I need you to come to me. In real life. Not this"—she gestured in a circle above her head—"whatever it is we get trapped in every night. I'm serious. I have the answer. It took twenty years, but *I have the answer!*"

"Come to you? Ridiculous. You won't give me specifics on where you live beyond 'north of the Starbond Sea.' I don't even know your last name." *I don't even know if you're real. What separates a hallucination from insanity from...this?*

Colors continued to run. The dream continued to blur. Mette became a watercolor of memory.

"We have to stop this. I don't think I can do it alone."

"Do *what* alone?"

"The party."

"What?" Her words made no sense. The dream dissolved to fragmented pigment. The smell of fried eggs and tomatoes saturated xir nose. Orin blanched and leaned back, determined to focus on the seeping wisp of Mette. From the range of silk and embroidered cotton nightgowns xie had seen Mette wear over the years, Orin had a good idea what kind of party she would attend. There would be silver cups and silver spoons, all imported from Earth. There would be big dresses, and jewels, and court apparel, because the only reason to take off a thick, embroidered nightgown was because you had something even more delicious to put on after. There might even be tiaras. Who knew how far up the social ladder Mette was? Regardless, Mette's parties would definitely not be the kind Orin could get into, even riding a dragon. Even riding a dragon with *lasers* on its head.

That was assuming Mette was even real.

Mette rushed her final, disembodied words, though the dream had faded to faint audio and Orin saw only darkness. "Three days from now. The Kingdom of Methalimus, past the Starbond Sea. South of the solar farm. It's a three-hour boat ride from End. Give any city wall guard you see your name and they'll let you through. Promise me, Orin, that you'll come. *Promise me.*"

"There is no way—"

The dream broke apart.

Orin crashed back into xir body. Xir eyes flew open.

A breakfast plate, still steaming, lay on Orin's bedside table. The smells tangled uncomfortably in Orin's head, mixing with Mette, and nightgowns, and the hope that maybe, *maybe*, Mette really had found the answer to their predicament.

Maybe...

Nope.

A floral morning breeze pushed past the shutters and blew the smell of eggs right back in Orin's face.

Xie leaned over the side of the bed and vomited.

* * *

"Heyyyyyy, you! Yes, you, the man in the hat with the...sculpture? Barrel? You sir, look like a man who could use buoyancy, and do I have the product for you!" Orin held up a glass beaker filled with a thick, milky substance. "Just a bit of home processing and you could float that barrel right down a river, regardless of contents! You could mudproof a dragon's foot! You could manufacture any number of prophylactics and guaranteed no skin irritation!" Orin flapped a hand in front of xir face and released a small handful of colorful rubber sequins into the now uncooperatively stale wind. "Possibilities," xie whispered loudly. "Endless."

The man in thick indigo-dyed cotton pants and shirt—bearded, bald, with a bit more green to his skin than Earth-normal—came over and wrinkled his nose at the bag. Red and blue sequins stuck to his pant legs, which wasn't wholly unusual at the second biggest market on the continent but occurred with far more frequency on the crafts side. However, since Orin supplied the sequins to the whole market, using them here was just good branding.

"What is it?" the man asked. His eyes flicked to Orin's face, and he frowned. "You okay? Rough couple nights?"

Orin swished xir hands from left to right, trying to pull his attention back to the plants and simultaneously trying to ward off a wave of dizziness. Thirty seconds of interaction with Mette always equated to half the night, and as much as Orin had grown accustomed to it all, just once, xie wanted a full night's sleep. And to keep breakfast down. And for Blathnaid to stop leaving breakfast on xir bedside table because as sweet as the gesture was, half the time the whole plate got ruined. Then Orin had no sleep *and* no breakfast, and looking like a hollowed-out pumpkin did nothing for market sales.

"I have a genetic condition and I've been up all night caring for these delightful plants so they would be in prime condition for today. Have a look."

Orin stepped to the side so the man could see the full table. A three-tiered shelf consumed the back half, filled with potted dandelions—some nearly as tall as xie was— that had budded but not yet bloomed. Thin, delicately spun glass tubes ran from the bottom of the pots into a trough on either side of the table, and a cloudier version of the 'blood' dripped from the ends. The front half of the table was neatly arranged, with perfectly measured bags of dandelion 'blood' threatening to congeal in the morning sunlight.

The man reluctantly moved his attention to the plants, poked one of the bags, and quickly drew his finger back when the substance rippled. "Is it alive?"

"Ah, no." Orin tossed the bag in xir hands at the man, who had to drop his barrel to catch it. Orin caught the barrel with a practiced smile for the practiced show. "It's a purity you'd need an HPLC to believe and it won *seven* awards at the End Upcoming Entrepreneurial Fair last year. Normally we're sold out by this time, but we brought a double batch and don't want to take the excess home. We can cut you a deal."

The man poked the bag again and wrinkled his nose. "Aren't these just common dandelions? The weed of the galaxy? And what is this? Latex? Chewing gum?"

Orin set the barrel down and tsked with xir hand. A few sequins still clung to xir palm and xie brushed them onto xir wrinkled linen pants. Xie'd pick them up later for resale, although it wouldn't matter if a few remained when Orin fell asleep. If Mette saw them, they'd be all she would talk about for a week. Sequins were much better emotion-free conversation than "'where do you live, come see me, hey maybe you're real and this isn't all a delusion want to sit in a fire and we'll see if extreme pain punts you from my brain?" Mette was always happy to talk about Orin's home, Orin's clothes, Orin's persistent financial situation. That Orin could never get the same from Mette just plain stunk of privilege, and money.

Orin wiped xir face with xir hands, hoping to rub the memory of Mette away, too. The sale mattered. Mette did not. "Latex from *lion fern*, sir. This is my specially bred variety, a delicate mix of Old Earth and native variants."

"The label here has it at twice the price of standard latex."

Orin went behind the booth and pulled out a thick sheet of cotton paper. "This has different properties though! The rubber is *unpuncturable* if manufactured correctly! The fluff seeds have similar properties *plus* they stick to anything, *and* I've had customers buy the plants just for the decorative value. Some have even claimed the seeds are medicinal! A lady in North End puts them on her child's scrapes for faster healing. I've got the purity report right here. If you take a look at the graphic—"

"Pass. At that price by weight, it'd be cheaper to import plastics from Earth. My cousin works for Galactic Shipping, Ltd. and can get me duty-free." He handed the bag back to Orin—more firmly than necessary—retrieved his barrel and walked away. His heels kicked up a little too high for Orin's liking. Pssh. Man didn't know an exceptional deal when it dropped into his hands. *Dandelions.* Seriously. Commonality didn't equate to uselessness.

A woman called out from the other side of the stand. "Hey, how much for the base plants?"

Orin put the paper down, squared xir shoulders, and turned around, another wide smile on xir face. "Ah, Miss, I have some lovely clippings in the back—"

The rush of the sale fell away and Orin lost xir breath. Xir skin broke out into a sweat. A familiar feeling—like xir brain was peeling from xir skull—settled in. Rushing blood thumped in xir ears, *bum pum bum pum.* The outline of the world blurred. Xie saw a glowing tulip-red hole, long, thin cylinders of glass, and unknown faces debating design xie didn't understand. There were leather-gloved hands. There was fire, fire, so much fire that it singed Orin's face, tickled xir nose hairs, and turned xir mouth to brittle dirt.

"They're, uh, just give me a minute." Orin nearly collapsed onto the brick street and took deep breaths of pig shit air. That was the stall next to xir's—the manure vendor. Excellent quality. Terrible smell, and a terrible time to visit Mette. The fantasies had a rough go of it during the day—or Orin's mind tried harder to fight them because xie wanted sales to afford a decent dinner. Xie also wanted to be a whole, independent person who didn't stumble around with headaches and nausea, and who got to sleep, *and* who could eat any food they wanted to because they still had enamel on their teeth.

Mette's hand caught something hot and while Orin couldn't see the offending item, xie still hissed in shared pain. "Damn it, Orin!" Mette hissed. "Get out of my head. Three days is when I want to see you, not while I'm working. Get out!"

Orin ignored Mette and tried to focus on xir potential customer. "Just a...another minute," Orin wheezed at the woman, who had already started to wander toward the pigs.

Then, just as suddenly as it came, the headache eased. The burning faded. Breath filled xir lungs and in a hop, Orin was back on xir feet. Xie brushed pieces of brick and a few shards of glass from xir pants and refused to admit defeat. "Miss! Won't you come and let me show you what these plants can do? I can offer a ten percent discount! Twenty, even, if you're buying bulk!"

The woman waved xir off with that concerned smile people always got when Orin had one of xir episodes. Xir smile bled away. The thrill of the sale ebbed, leaving only the residual headache and a memory of blistered skin, and a thirst no amount of water ever seemed to quench. Orin cursed. Xir mind always jumped to that fantasy realm at the absolute worst times. The woman and the man had been the first customers to come down this row in, four hours? Five? Half of the day had passed and xir shelves were still full. The crowds stubbornly remained slow and thin. Orin didn't need to be daydreaming about fantasy women and fire.

Fantasy. Mette had to be a fantasy, Orin reasoned for the millionth time, because every single person Orin had ever chanced speaking to about xir condition had said so. Everybody laughed, too. Researchers at the university laughed. Soothsayers laughed. Witches, magicians, herbalists, old men telling fairy stories at the market edges to earn a few coins, all laughed.

Orin didn't need laughter. Xie needed sales. Now.

End's Market ran twice per month—the space was used as a food cart plaza otherwise—and was the biggest market this side of the Starbond Sea. The only bigger one, in fact, was the one in Methalimus inside the gated city, which was likely why Orin's imagination had finally decided that was where Mette was from. Who didn't dream of selling at the Methalimus market? Of course, vending at both major markets was tightly controlled and one had to apply through a jury selection.

Orin could hack it at End with small-batch dandelion latex. It made *really, really* good rubber (or rubber sequins) and since they didn't manufacture any petrochemicals on the planet, the sticky seeds of this variety—*Orin's* variety—were used for exterior texturing on buildings and, by at least one customer, for scrapbooking. Xie had never verified the medicinal properties, but it was high on xir list for the next time xie had a monetary surplus.

Those applications at Methalimus Market? There was no way, even if the reports on healing came back positive. Orin had applied the past five years in a row. Xie'd received a form rejection each time. And the people of Methalimus were supposed to be open minded, too. It was the only major city on their continent supporting the showing and practice of magic. What could they possibly have against a few harmless dandelions?

"Bad day, then? You want to close early and get food?" Blathnaid knocked his hand against Orin's temple while xie stared at the small cluster of people bartering for a fat piglet.

Orin turned and exhaled forcibly enough to vibrate xir lips. Blathnaid, Orin's only childhood friend, stood a head taller than Orin but had the same thick musculature. His hair though, was hellebore green—a mutation the original planetary colonists hadn't had, and that no one could adequately explain. It only occurred in those born in End, and in the gated city of Methalimus. He hadn't gotten the corresponding purple-green melanin mutation at least, and his skin was a perfectly human light brown. They both wore linen clothes as neither could afford cotton, which meant they both looked perpetually wrinkled.

"Crap day. You see any big crowds at the main entry?"

"Nope. Dead as an Earth horse out there. Everyone's doing their shopping at Methalimus this cycle, so they have a shot at seeing the coronation. It's in...two days, I think? Three? Yeah."

Orin slumped into a two-legged chair, which immediately threatened to topple. "Well, there goes my food budget. Crickets it is."

"Nah, I can help." He thumped his chest pocket. From behind him, a rabbit startled, then hopped off to wallow with the nearby pigs.

"You already pay all the rent, Blathnaid. You shouldn't have to do food, too. And please stop making me breakfast. Please."

"Meh. I don't mind. Besides, we can always eat those dandelion leaves—"

Orin kicked him halfheartedly in the shin. Blathnaid gave a mock yelp but grinned. "Leave the *lion ferns* alone. They're the wave of the future."

"You make twice on sequins than what you do on selling raw latex. I still think you should move over to the craft section and broaden your client base."

"I hate you."

Blathnaid almost cut a retort—xie could see it in the smirk of his eyes—then opted for a different tone. "Not a lot of future if you die in the present, Orin. You have to eat." They both hadn't had to worry about eating much, not recently, but it was plenty easy to remember xir and Blathnaid's childhood as errand boys for the markets—first the small ones then, as they got older and quicker, the big ones like End. Easy, too, to remember how people's tips didn't buy more than a meal a day, and how the roof in the barn where they were allowed to sleep leaked badly, especially in monsoon season. At least the market was airy and cool— the bamboo and oiled tarps keeping the worst of the sun and rain off, and the brick roads keeping the insects at bay. With hundreds of vendors at any given time, the stalls stacked row upon row in an endless yawn of commerce.

Aside from Blathnaid, it was the best part of Orin's life. Not that xie could have held any other kind of job. Not with Mette in xir head.

"Yeah. Fine." Xie stood and pulled a thick, insulated box from under the display table. "Help me get the plants packed back up and we can go."

"Or, you could talk to this guy first." Blathnaid stepped back behind Orin. A young man, perhaps twenty, stood a handspan from the edge of the display. Nothing about him was extraordinary, not his walnut-bark brown hair and skin, nor his yellow-brown eyes or fitted denim jacket that spoke of comfort but not wealth.

Orin *knew* him.

They'd never met before, xie was certain. He wasn't a former customer or patron, and he was too young to have hired xir or Blathnaid when they were younger. His clothes didn't distinguish his home country at all, but Orin knew if he smiled, xie would see his bottom teeth out of alignment. Knew he had a dimple in his chin and another on his right cheek. Knew he paid in notes and not credit, even for big orders.

"I was wondering about the plants," he said, and his voice sounded exactly like Orin knew it would. Snappy, like when you kicked a field dandelion just right and the flower head popped off.

Orin reached over and pinched Blathnaid, who swallowed his surprised squeak with a burp. Then he pinched xir back, hard enough that xir eyes watered.

"L-lion fern." Orin straightened and tried to reset. Xie knew him from Mette, but Mette wasn't real, and this man clearly was. Therefore, having this reaction was unnecessary. "Sir, may I introduce lion fern, a robust new variant on an old tradition. If you'll look to your side"—xie pointed at the left bucket, half filled with white dandelion 'blood'—"you'll see the purest latex known to the planet. It has superior rubber potential. Great for small-batch, high-end processing, with endless uses in both the life sciences and astrobiological arts. Could I interest you in a free sample?"

"I'd like a case of the plants, please, or however many you're willing to sell me." The man reached into his jacket and pulled out a singular note, stamped with the potentate's— the current diplomatic figurehead of the northern hemisphere—face.

He paid with those a lot, write-in notes that could have any value the vendor wrote on them. Orin knew that. Xie *knew* it was coming but seeing the note—the potentate's bored yellow eyes faded into the pink background of the cotton paper—xie still couldn't believe it.

Blathnaid's eyes bugged from their sockets and Orin had to restrain xirself from snatching the note and running away. That kind of money was a proper house for Blathnaid and xir, with running water and electricity and a full fridge.

It was all that *plus* a ticket to Methalimus, first class. If xie wanted to believe in midnight dream women.

"Any amount you think is fair," the man said, placing the note on the display and anchoring it with the edge of a clay pot.

"Sir, we would *love* to box these plants for you. Won't you please have a seat?" Blathnaid pulled Orin's chair around and offered it to the man, who nodded his head and sat.

"Snap out of it," Blathnaid hissed as he pulled Orin back behind the tall wall of dandelions and pointed to an empty box. "If it's Mette tell her to shove off until we get the order finished."

Orin nodded absently as xie packed vegetable foam around a pot, then slid another wrapped pot next to it in the box.

"How many do you want to give him? You have like twenty more at home, right?"

"Yeah. Give him everything." Orin stood and handed the first filled box to the man. "Did you have a vehicle around here, sir? Dragon cart, maybe?" The only mammals bigger than pigs that had survived the trip from Earth were humans. The colonists had gotten creative, especially with plants. The only Earth import that hadn't needed genetic modification to grow on their world had been dandelions. The introduced varieties had immediately interbred with the natives, and the five species that had originally come from Earth looked so similar to the three on the new planet that very few people, including Orin, could routinely tell them apart with a magnifying lens.

"Just around. Give me a minute and I'll be back. We can load then. And thank you." He gave a soft salute, skirted the pigs and their mud, and disappeared behind a booth selling lichen dyes.

"They'll get smashed if he takes them by dragon cart." Blathnaid shoved the last pot into a slot that was just a hair too small for it. The edge of the cardboard ripped.

"Not our problem. I just want him gone."

Blathnaid taped the corner of the box and leaned against the display. He puckered his lips to the side in a sort of funny frown. "What's going on?"

"Nothing."

"Liar. Normally I can't get you to *stop* talking. Do I have to get you drunk?"

"You can't afford to get me drunk."

"Can." Again he tapped his pocket, and pitched his voice down low. "Last gig tipped well because I'm a maaaaster illusionist. Plus, they feed me their signature dinner. Another reason to perform there. It's exhausting, I'm exhausted, but it's worth it. I just wish I didn't have to reveal my 'secret' at the end of every show to prove it's not magic."

Orin couldn't bring xirself to smile, even knowing how much Blathnaid loved mashed strawberry bake, and practicing illegal magic. "I just...know him. You know?"

Blathnaid raised an eyebrow. "Sex? Sales? Robbery?" His eyes narrowed and a mischievous smile spread across his face. "Please tell me it was sex."

Orin tapped xir temple.

"Oh. Fuck."

The *thunk thunk* of rubber wheels over potholes drew both of their attentions down the brick lane. A wood cart wide enough to hold twice the stock Orin was providing jostled between the few remaining shoppers. The wood planks had a fresh coat of red stain, and the wheels were definitely new. The Komodo dragons that pulled the thing were *not*, and Orin could hear their labored breathing from half a block away.

"Weird guy," Blathnaid said with a shake of his head. "He's got Methalimus notes—*blank* Methalimus notes—yet he drives a cart with dragons that look old enough to have come over with the original settlers from Earth and are clearly not well trained. No way they'd pass inspection and get licensed for transit. And his jacket has gold thread woven into the cuffs. Did you see that? Like spider silk or something. Like he's got some awesome job but doesn't want us to *think* he has an awesome job, but is concurrently too ridiculous to realize that handing us a note like that screams 'I work for Methalimus government, live in the gated city, and can afford mashed strawberry for every meal because I'm fancy and rich.'"

The cart stopped close to Orin's stall. The dragons strained against their ropes, their forked tongues licking the pig shit smell from the air. Blathnaid began loading the cart before the man hopped from his seat. Orin pocketed the note. It was always possible he might change his mind.

"If you need more, sir, please do let me know. My contact information is stamped onto the bottom of every pot. I take electronic communications and carrier pigeon, if you prefer."

The man grabbed the last box and pushed it up against the others in the back of the cart. He handed Blathnaid a five-mark, the usual currency, and nodded in thanks. "Will see how these go and get back to you. Put anything you think is fair on the note. The auditors check, but not closely. Thank you, Mister?" He frowned, likely trying to decide where to kiss Orin. Left for women, right for men. Forehead for everyone else.

Orin pointed to xir forehead.

"Ah!" He stepped into Orin and briefly kissed Orin's hairline. He'd have had to stoop to get any lower. Orin kissed his right cheek. "I'll be in touch, Orin."

"Sir?" Orin called after him as he climbed back onto his wagon and tried to convince his dragons that the pigs were too expensive a lunch. "Your name, if I may? For customer service and to let you know about sales? Do you have a card or chip I could scan?"

The dragons started forward and at least two ceramic pots broke in the process. Orin cringed. The man pulled the dragons to a halt. "Sir Minjae. I'm under direct contract with Lady Lorimette. The dandelions are set to seed in a few days, correct?"

Orin squinted. *Lorimette?* No. That was ridiculous. Xie nodded. "Yes, sir. Their flowers are only just opening. This variety seeds in four days, sometimes a day or so faster. You can force the processes with a sharp blast of heat if you have a small acetylene torch handy. But I have seed bags if that's what you're looking for. You'll be able to plant them more quickly or I have the raw seeds with the sticky latex still on them if you're looking for decoration?"

The man stroked one of the dandelion leaves. "She's still debating magic at the ceremony so I'm not sure yet how we want the plants. The lady wants the seeds in plant form for the start of the coronation, anyway. She's got a dream of walking back out after the ceremony in a shower of petals, but dandelion fluff will work just as well. The heat opening varieties are hard to find. They'll survive repotted in glass for a few days? Our purchaser made a mistake and ordered three hundred and twenty-two glass pots instead of ceramic. They're all we've got. And a few of them are massive and big enough to shove a body into. If we don't find a way to use them, Lady Lorimette will recuperate the money with a mass firing."

Glass pots? No, that didn't matter. What did matter was that the future queen might not want magic at her coronation? Methalimus was *built* on magic. The city had a whole damn library with devoted texts. They had universities where scholars studied magic. Blathnaid's dream from the day they'd met had been to double major in herbalism and incantation at Methalimus School for the Mystic Arts. Methalimus was called the Gated City because the city wall was made entirely of shale, carved with magic runes. Avoiding magic in Methalimus was literally impossible. Magic had no discernable rules, and the entire rest of the planet had washed their hands of it. But Methalimus—Methalimus was where you went to *bathe* in it.

End was where you went if you wanted to completely avoid magic, which of course just pushed it to the black market, but whatever. It wasn't like magic didn't exist in End. People just ignored it the way one might ignore a mildly pungent odor. And if this guy wanted to buy dandelions, what did xie care what he did with them? "Yeah, whatever you want to pot them in is fine. Lion ferns are robust in the short term." Xie squinted at the man. "You could also—"

The man made a shooing motion, snapped the reins, and the cart lurched down the road. The sound of cracking ceramic pots filled the air.

Orin watched the cart lurch down the street, cringing with every broken pot. "Blathnaid, did you know my lion ferns have a reputation in Methalimus? I wonder if someone bought one, cloned it, and is selling it there?" Xie frowned and felt the tips of xir ears turn red. "My strain is patented. If I get a name..."

Blathnaid put a hand on Orin's shoulder and clucked as the dragons lunged at a stall of piglets. "Orin, I love you dearly, but no one cares about your dandelions outside of wanting some greenery in their house. They were weeds on Earth, and they're weeds here. There isn't a field they don't grow in, native, imported, or hybridized. They're dandelions. I know for a fact that the tall, skinny variety weaves itself through gaps in the stone wall of Methalimus. You can pick a dandelion anywhere on this continent. That makes this purchase unusual."

Orin weighed the next words, and the likelihood of Blathnaid laughing, before speaking. The thought was ridiculous but then again, so was having an imaginary friend you couldn't get to leave. That thought didn't slow Orin's frantically beating heart. "Do you think it's Mette?"

"Huh?"

Orin shrugged, pretending xie didn't care when in fact the prospect of Mette orchestrating the event was *terrifying*. "You know. Maybe Mette is trying to get me to Methalimus?"

Blathnaid cocked his head. "Are we taking dream woman seriously now? Did you send me a note via pigeon and then the pigeon got eaten, conveniently, by a dragon? Or are we going to go steal more magic texts from traveling carts and fall asleep reading them just so we do a spell wrong, and you end up losing all your hair again? Or I break my leg fishing you from the bottom of a pond you've tried to drown yourself in? I thought we settled this, Orin. Mette isn't real and if she was real, there's nothing you can do about her popping into your head that doesn't involve you dying."

"No. Yes. This is different. Hear me out. Think about it. Lori*mette*?" A weight dropped in Orin's stomach as xie worked through the details. Xie felt the familiar nausea rise up, though Mette's presence was nowhere near. She was wealthy, yes. But a princess? Really? With that kind of money, Mette could have made a real difference in Orin's life. In Orin and Blathnaid's lives. Instead, she'd kept her location hidden until...until she was sure she could get herself separated from Orin?

"Orin—"

"Lorimette. *Lady.* As in, about to go through the coronation ceremony in Methalimus to become princess under our potentate. Coincidence? I think not."

"Okay." Blathnaid leaned against the booth frame. "Coronation is just a fancy word for a party, so this makes her rich as all get-out? This would also explain how a man purchasing for the coronation knows about you and your no-name dandelion lion fern even though Methalimus and End are separated by the Starbond Sea. The only thing our two cities have in common is being comically overrun by dandelions. But does Mette being rich help us? I'm all ears if it does. But I still don't think Mette is real."

"I..." Orin had told Mette about the market, and living in End, but never the lion fern dandelions. There'd never been enough time and they had *rules.* Unspoken, sure, but they'd both learned that trying to convince people you wanted to meet the phantom in your head got you absolutely nowhere, so what was the point of tormenting each other with details? Or trying to explain the mechanics of dandelion husbandry? Never mind that the disorientation and nausea and the whole floating-above-your-own-body thing always got in the way of deeper introspection.

Orin sucked in a deep breath. Pig shit air did wonders for grounding you in the moment.

Blathnaid poked xir in the ribs. "What are you going to do?"

Orin sat on the lowest shelf of the display and watched the cart turn around a corner at the edge of the market, and out of sight. The blank note lay crumpled in xir pocket. What had Mette said? She could fix them? Fix them at a *party* maybe?

What hadn't they tried already? Orin had already visited every soothsayer, herbalist-witch, illegal magician, and doctor this side of the Starbond Sea. They'd all agreed that it wasn't real, but if it was real, it'd have been magic, and that kind of magic didn't exist. It didn't exist on Earth, and it definitely didn't exist on their planet. But Mette lived in the Gated City. Magic was allowed—even celebrated—in the Gated City. Maybe she'd found a new text. Maybe she'd found a practitioner. Maybe she had another half-baked, life-threatening plan that would end up crippling xir, and then Blathnaid would have to manage Orin's lion fern business because the world needed sequins and rubber. Maybe...

No.

It didn't matter one way or the other. If there was even a chance of finally getting a full night's sleep, being rid of the smell of fire and feeling of tight callouses, of the sight of old leather and scratchy wool and Mette's hovering, nightgown-clad form, of not puking every damn night....

No matter how small or silly or potentially dangerous meeting Mette might be, Orin had to go. Xie would be free of Mette, even if it killed them both.

Chapter 2

"You could have just sent a ticket. Your man wasn't subtle. Not that I mind the money but dragons? In an End market?" Orin's consciousness hovered over Mette's bed—an ash four-poster with a coarse silk canopy. Mette's phantom sat just to the left of her actual body. She appeared to have fallen asleep directly after...work? Her cotton pants and shirt had dark smudges across them, and a pair of glassworkers' protective glasses perched atop her head. Odd work, for a princess, but royalty probably needed hobbies to keep busy.

Mette eyed her sleeping body. "Orin, as usual, I don't know what you're talking about." She rubbed absently at the burn on her hand. Orin rubbed xir own, the memory of pain making xir wince.

"Could you stop touching hot things, too? It's hard to land a sale when your hand lights up with imaginary fire."

Mette scowled at the apparition that was Orin. "Why are you such a grouch tonight?"

The five hours between the end of the market and bed had been enough time for Orin to actually consider the mechanics of traveling to a city to which xie had never been; to meet a woman xie had only met in dreams. It had also given Orin time to think about Mette—*really* think about her—and her station, her access to information Orin didn't have, and what attending the coronation meant for a mid-tier dandelion seller from End.

"I'm grumpy because it could take days to cash that note. We have two banks within a day's walking distance in End and they're both closing early for the coronation. How are Blathnaid and I supposed to get supplies? And added to that, how long have you known where I live? Why didn't you tell me where *you* lived? Did you think I was going to come to your door and rob you?!" Orin rubbed xir stomach, imitating Mette, who looked like she had just swallowed bile. Pressure was building at the base of xir skull, heralding an epic headache come morning.

"Orin I...don't even know what you *sell*. How could I possibly know where you live? If this is about money, look I...I'm trying to work out how I can get you passage on a ship to get to Methalimus. Please, don't be mad! I really think this will work."

Orin felt the tightness on xir skin that heralded the end of their visit. "I still don't like how you went about all this. I mean, you could have told me."

"I've barely told you a thing and you're already mad at me!"

Orin turned from her and the dream dissolved. Then, like every night for the past twenty odd years, xie woke up, leaned over the side of the bed, and vomited in Blathnaid's lovingly prepared breakfast eggs.

* * *

"I can't believe you're turning down a soon-to-be queen. Financially this is a terrible decision. I just want you to know that. I thought about this all night. There's money to be made here, Orin. So, so much money."

Blathnaid and Orin debated as they sat on branchwood chairs in front of a pushcart fruit juice vendor, whose booth space Orin shared when the market ran. Clouds choked the blue from the sky overhead, their grey souring Orin's mood and the juice.

"She's using me," Orin retorted after swallowing a mouthful of a pineapple-rose apple blend. "Can't you see that?"

"Do you care?" Blathnaid countered. "Okay I mean, clearly you do, but should you?"

Orin crossed xir arms and sat back in the chair. "Up until yesterday you thought she was imaginary just as much as I did."

"Only because we didn't have any real information. Now we do. There's so much more to magic than what we see illegally in End. Mette's a lady-princess-almost-*queen*. She's probably read the whole damn magic library they have in the city center and figured this entire business out. Maybe she has a degree! Did you think of that?" His eyes turned starry. "Like in...apparitions or sleep walking. But she hasn't mastered it yet and that's why she keeps slipping into your head. But now her professor, who has like a long Merlin beard and wears a pointy hat, made her do a literature review and she found a way to stop it."

"Blathnaid, I don't think—"

He leaned in and clinked the rim of his glass against Orin's. "When I did errands for Fen the Magician, some of the stuff he had me fetch him...I mean, I *saw* magic, Orin. Unicorns live in the southern continent. I've touched horn. Fen can levitate with six words and a drink that smells like molasses. Mind sleepwalking isn't outside the realm of possibility, and magic isn't just parlor tricks. Do you know what they had to do to strawberries to get them to grow here?" He pointed to his green hair. "It's not just that this world has magic, it's that we interact with magic, every day. We *consume* it. Magic does things to people. We can pretend Earth scientists solved all of this planet's growing problems with CRISPER DNA sequences, but Fen knew better. It took magic. And it got inside us, and it's changing us, the humans. Benign effects might be the norm, but life mutates. Your link with Mette, if it's real, that's not a wholly unexpected level. But"—he took a deep breath and slammed a fist down on the table—"if your brain is linked to future royalty, no matter how figureheady she is, let's not pass up a chance to live in a house with fancy wool carpet instead of plank flooring. Think about it. Green hair gets stares. Mind links get...I don't have a good rhyme. But money. They get money."

Orin stuck out xir tongue. "It's too convenient to make jokes. Why now? Why after two decades? She's going to be a queen. You don't think that's a little suspicious?"

"Do *you* want to keep puking every night, and eating budget crickets twice a month when the market is low? *I* think they're pretty delicious, personally, but I know you hate those hairy little legs." He ran fingertips up Orin's arms.

"Ack! Stop it." Xie batted his hand away and scooted xir chair to the opposite end of the round table. "You and I worked for rich people long enough already. We're supposed to be going away from that, not back toward it."

Blathnaid smirked. "Yeah, but I'd do it for a pretty woman in a nightgown."

"I *never* said she was pretty."

"You didn't have to."

Orin ground xir knuckles into the side of the chair. "Just conceptualize this with me for a minute. I travel out of End. No, *we* travel out of End because I want another pair of eyes to confirm I'm not hallucinating. We travel out of End—which opted against figurehead royalty during colonization and works just fine as a free market with a handful of big farms—to Methalimus, where people get excited over titles? Are we title people? *Magic* people? Is that who we are now?"

Blathnaid raised an eyebrow. "We're *money* people. All those things usually come in tandem."

"Yeah, fine. You're not wrong." Orin looked back at the thin juice lady, debating another glass. "I'll leave the market early today and try to catch the bank before it closes. I'll take out enough to get us both passage on the next trans-sea ship. We can afford one of the jet ones, with this thing." Xie tapped the rim of xir glass, trying to catch the vendor's attention. "Hey, miss, could I try the mangosteen?"

The woman looked up from her juicer, started to smile, then froze. The glass fell from her hands and broke on the brick road. Orin looked down the street to where she pointed. A wooden stagecoach, pulled by six heaving Komodo dragons clipped down the road. The carriage swung wildly from side to side, knocking over shuttered stalls as it did. The fruit vendor kicked the locks off her cart's wheels and hurriedly pushed it off the road and into the sedge of a field, motioning for Orin and Blathnaid to follow.

"Come on." Orin pulled the back of Blathnaid's shirt while xir friend stood on the side of the road, mouth agape. Dragons, rather, that many dragons all at once, was more accumulated wealth than all of End, and it was so unnecessary. Orin shook xir head. They were a giant pain all around, and far too often penned in fields that would be better suited to wildflower cultivation. They were ornery, they looked ridiculous, and no one in End used stagecoaches. End didn't upkeep its brick roads enough.

"Blathnaid, come on." Xie jerked this time and Blathnaid fell back, hard enough to land them both on their backsides. They scooched backward as quickly as they could. The dragons continued, close enough now that Orin could see the speckling inside their pinkish mouths and throats. They were on good, leather leashes but still had a *lot* of teeth.

One of the dragons emitted a deep, throaty growl that sounded like an Earth gasoline engine. Orin's stomach did a flip. Xie could see the lead dragon was longer than xie was tall and suddenly a dandelion field seemed like an excellent place for a dragon to be. Anywhere, really, as long as it wasn't right in xir face.

"This is how we die," Blathnaid said. "Smothered in disgusting dragon breath and Orin, they have very pointy teeth. Did you know that?" Their butts hit the edge of the sedge as they continued their frantic scramble backward. The seat of Orin's pants immediately turned wet. Xie looked down to find xirself at the edge of a pile of pig droppings, as fresh smelling today as they'd been yesterday.

The driver pulled the dragons, miraculously, to a halt just as Orin thought xie could smell their metallic breath, and just as the wetness from the grass and shit finished saturating xir pants.

"What the hell?" Blathnaid tried to ease his breathing.

Orin thought xie saw the curtain on the main front window wiggle. Xie caught a flash of dark hair and then xir stomach knotted. The throbbing started at the base of xir skull, rekindling xir early morning headache. Xie hunched over, face between xir knees, and swallowed bile.

"Tell Mette now isn't a good time!"

"Not the same," Orin managed through gritted teeth. This time the nausea came with double vision. Orin could see the inside of the stagecoach—its plain lacquer interior, the style of the molding around the window—as well as the green-brown muck beneath xir feet. The gaze inside the coach shifted and Orin saw worn, brown leather boots that ended just above the ankle, thick, blue cotton pants, and fingers clenched in the fabric.

A slightly-damp hand grasped Orin's shoulder. "Hey," Blathnaid said, his voice filled with concern. "What's wrong? Is it not Mette? Is it the smell?"

"Stagecoach," Orin managed to say as xir vision layered the multicolored grass over leather boots. "Can you help me get there?"

"I don't really think that's a good idea, Orin." This time it wasn't concern, and it wasn't gentle ribbing. Blathnaid has used that tone maybe four times in their shared lives, and every time, he'd been right.

Orin ignored him and used Blathnaid's shoulder to stand, took one quick look at xir backside, and decided to try to forget the unfortunate staining there.

"Orin," Blathnaid cautioned, a hand on xir shoulder as he stood as well.

Talking was no longer an option. If Orin opened xir mouth, only breakfast juice would come out. Instead, xie stalked to the stagecoach, grabbed the handle and threw the door open.

On the other side stood Mette—just as green around the gills, but positively seeping regal authority.

Mette grabbed onto Orin's shirt and hauled xir into the coach. "Shut up and get in. You too—whatever your name is—if you want. I'm sorry about this. But I need your help and I don't have time to argue. And..." she pinched the bridge of her freckled nose and covered her mouth with her other hand. "What is it you sell? You smell like shit."

Chapter 3

Mette was real.

Orin didn't move from the seat xie'd been thrust into. Xie couldn't move. What did one say to their dream-phantom woman? Clearly puking on her was not an option, though still a possibility. The nausea ebbed the longer Orin stared at Mette but refused to recede entirely.

Mette's familiar head of brown hair was mussed instead of in its usual coils, but otherwise, she was exactly as she'd appeared in every dream Orin had ever had. And here, in person, Orin couldn't pretend the way her mouth turned down into a half frown, or the fine dusting of freckles across her right cheek, didn't make xir wish their connection was something…useful.

The stomach sickness rolled back and the headache eased but Mette—in daylight, in the sounds and smells of the real world—Orin's brain couldn't process it all.

Real.

"You look…tangible." Mette stumbled over the last word, grasping at their shared reality. "Do you…always smell like this?" She pulled at the armpit of her shirt. "I always look like this, if you were wondering the same."

Orin tried to ignore her stained, torn clothes and worn boots, to focus on Mette's flushed face. Though they'd been on the road for nearly half an hour without speaking to this point—an uncanny length of time to spend staring at a nighttime specter—Mette still sucked in air like she was about to drown. Blathnaid did his best to give them space, though Orin knew there was only so long he could look out the window before he'd feel compelled to speak.

The interior of the stagecoach smelled of fresh lacquer, which barely covered the smell of poop. Orin had expected more frills, but inside was mostly flat wood, with just a bit of detail on the molding. The curtains were black linen, and the thin cushions on the benches were a coarse spun silk and looked homemade. A small plastic cooler—vintage from Earth— wedged against the wall opposite the door. On top of the cooler, strapped to the thing with a strip of brown leather, was a worn book with a library bar code up the spine. It all clashed horribly with the volume of dragons tearing them down the road.

It wasn't until after a particularly vicious pothole wherein all three of them whacked their heads on the ceiling that Mette found her voice again. "So. Hey." She rubbed her head and made an attempt to square her shoulders. Orin noticed wrinkles in the cotton across Mette's chest and midsection, and frowned. Orin and Blathnaid didn't have the best clothes in End, but what they had—when it wasn't covered in filth—was still better quality and better fitting than what Mette was wearing.

Mette filled her clothes out a bit better than either of them, too, but that was beside the point.

"It's, um, good to see you," mumbled Mette. "In the flesh. I'm still working on the smell."

Orin crossed xir arms and slid xir bottom against the cushioned seat, making a horrible *squelllllch* sound. "You dragged me into a stagecoach. When I didn't answer you that night, I didn't mean come and get me."

Mette paled. "I have answers, Orin. I just want you to hear me out. If you say no after, I'll pay for your passage back to the market on a fancy air jet. I promise. I'll even buy you a bath."

Orin lifted xir left cheek from the bench with a *slupp.* "Look at me. Look at us. You *dragged me into a stagecoach.*"

Mette crossed her arms as well, and sat back in a humph.

They were back to this again—weird telepaths with shitty communication skills. Twenty years seemed like an eternity, in that moment. If every night they saw each other for seconds, how many hours had they spent together overall? What did xie actually know about Mette? She liked glasswork? She had fancy nightgowns? She could afford dragon carriages?

She was going to be a queen. Right?

"Of all the weird magic in the world, I had to share my head with a freaking princess."

"A princess?" Mette's lip curled and she sat forward. "Wait, you share your mind with a princess? It's not just me?"

"Well, soon to be queen. Whatever you want to call yourself now."

Mette uncrossed her legs. She looked at Blathnaid first, maybe for help, but he shook his head and held up his hands. "Oh, no. I've got no pigs in this race. I'm here because Orin pays half the rent—well, *should* pay half the rent—so if xie decides we help you, we help you. If xie decides we beat you unconscious and take your stagecoach, we'll do that."

Mette looked increasingly horrified. "I'm...I work in a glass factory, Orin. It cost me three months' wages to come here."

This time Orin looked at Blathnaid. "But, you wanted me to come to the coronation, right?" Orin asked. "The coronation for Princess Lorimette. Mette. You sent that guy to buy my plants. I figured you wanted a gardener or something after you separated our brains."

Mette's mouth fell open. "Guy... Wait. No! I don't want you to be my servant! Orin, you and I are...never mind. I found a book, Orin, on this thing. I broke into the Royal Library. Well, I was let in to repair one of their older glass sculptures and I 'got lost' looking for the bathroom. I wandered to the magic section. I browsed. I maybe didn't properly check this book out. The mechanics are irrelevant." She pointed first at her temple, then at Orin's. "I can separate us, but I need your help to do it because there's a lot of fire involved. It's complicated. I'm not soon-to-be Princess Lorimette, whom I have never met, by the way, although I'll grant you that our names are similar—it's a common name in Methalimus— and I never sent anyone anywhere."

"What?" Orin asked. "You are clearly a princess." Xie tilted xir head, and again inspected the worn boots and frayed edges of Mette's pants. "Right? A...rough and tumble princess?"

"Nope, I think she's really a glass worker and this is so much more interesting. So." Blathnaid scooted closer to Orin. Orin watched him try to suppress a grin, and fail miserably. Xie didn't blame him. The situation was quickly becoming absolutely ridiculous. "You stole a book, then you stole Orin. Is the stagecoach also stolen by chance?"

"Borrowed," Mette countered. "Don't ask about the dragons."

"Borrowed with permission?" Orin asked.

"You know, that's really a grey area if you think about it."

"Okay let's not." Orin rapped on the ceiling and, as xie'd hoped, the stagecoach drew to a stop. "You're not a princess, you have Blathnaid's grip on morality, and you really live inside my head and in real life. Fine." It was not fine, but the fastest way out of a stinking stagecoach was not with arguing. "You didn't send someone to buy all my plants?"

"No," said Mette. "Why would I want your plants?"

"Shut it. Everyone needs lion fern. Regardless, what, exactly, did you pay for here?"

Mette folded her hands in her lap and took a deep breath. "Sea passage on one of the jet boats, and the driver up front for the stagecoach. I couldn't afford jets for both, and I don't know how to run dragons. Could I ask who he is? I didn't plan on a third, although an extra hand will help."

Blathnaid cut in before Mette could answer. "I'm Blathnaid, which is a word from Earth that means 'flower,' and I'm guessing my parents either decided it was an old family name that needed use or wanted a girl. It doesn't bother me because my name doesn't affect the length of my, uh, 'stamen.'" He waved his hands mildly at his waist.

Orin sighed. Blathnaid ignored xir. "Parents died. I met Orin here when we were six, picking dandelion leaves for soup on some farmer's feral lot. Orin puked on me our first night sleeping next to each other in a barn." He pointed at Mette. "Your fault, by the way. I got to hear all about xir first dream with you in it. We've been together ever since. I make xir eggs every morning because one of these mornings xie is going to wake up and you won't be there, and there will be this amazing breakfast waiting, and a new life just beyond that."

"Blathnaid," Orin said. "That's...really sweet. But we could maybe wait on the eggs until after the separation? There's no need to constantly ruin them. Everything else is already such a mess. Breakfast doesn't need to be."

"This isn't my fault you know," said Mette.

"Yeah, but it isn't Orin's either. And Orin, I hear you on the eggs, and I respectfully decline your suggestion."

Orin knew when xie'd lost a battle. And they needed to get moving again. The stench was unbearable. "Do you vomit after every dream, too?" Orin asked Mette.

She nodded. "I sleep with a bucket by my bed. Sometimes I puke during the daytime ones, too."

"Yeah, those are worse."

"And you...sell?" Mette asked Orin and Blathnaid. "Lions? I'm sorry, I'm still not clear on what you sell. I heard someone talking about End Market yesterday during our daytime connection and I just, came. I had to."

Blathnaid ran a hand through his short hair, preening. "*I* am an illusionist. Mostly I do card tricks but whatever brings in the money."

"He makes rabbits disappear by mashing them into hidden pockets in hats," Orin added.

"I can do real magic, I'm just not licensed yet and I can't afford passage to Methalimus, where I won't be strung up for it. And, if you give away an illusionist's secrets, then it isn't any fun, Orin."

"I don't think it's ever fun for the rabbits. Anyway, Blathnaid is a friend. The only friend I've got, really, because you can only puke on someone so many times before they run screaming."

Mette chuckled and Orin watched the edges of her eyes crinkle with her smile.

"I'm Orin. Same deal as Blathnaid, mostly. Dead parents. An aunt raised me for a few years before she died, too. She farmed and taught me the foundations of dandelion farming. Now I, uh, sell lion fern blood."

Blathnaid snickered.

Orin glared at him.

"My parents were farmers too, before the Dragon Drought about thirty years back. They switched to glass work. What is a lion fern?" Mette asked. Her genuine interest was unexpected. There was no reason that Orin needed to impress her, but that information didn't seem to be reaching xir mouth. Thank dragons Mette wasn't a princess. Falling for a glass worker was much more in line with Orin's life goals of not being incarcerated for harassing royalty.

"My own wildflower variant, bred for exceptional purity of blood, with some light analgesic properties in the fluff. In just the right soil—"

"Xie milks dandelions for low-yield latex."

Orin flushed. "What was that about secrets, Blathnaid?"

"We're not trying to make a sale! Let's finish the introductions before the dragons eat us."

They had zero percent chance of being eaten by domesticated Komodo dragons. Orin sniffed. "The blood, latex, whatever, has a lot of applications."

"Mmm," Mette hummed, smiling. "I'm sure it does. I also think this is the longest conversation we've ever had."

It was far too warm in the stagecoach.

"Your turn," Orin managed. "Elaborate."

"Mette Wong. I have parents, both living, both of whom work in the glass factory. Before that we were farmers, as I said, for seven generations, going back to the original colonists, so I know your trade a bit, Orin, even if the farm died before I was born. Dunno what they grew. Strawberries maybe. But they've got photos from when you couldn't go outside without crushing dandelion. The things choked all the photos, so thickly you can't tell what their crops actually were. My parents went bankrupt when mom was about four months pregnant with me. But I was six as well the first time, with the dream." She looked down at her leather shoes. "I used to try to convince them that Orin existed. Tales from a wide-eyed six-year-old are pretty easy to dismiss, it seems. Eventually, they had me convinced as well. Until recently."

"We got it into our heads to walk until we found you, once," Orin said. Sufficiently convinced Mette wasn't going to murder them or sell them or offer them as a sacrifice at Lady Lorimette's coronation, xie knocked again on the roof of the stagecoach, and it jostled forward again. "No money for jets or carriages, of course, so we did it by foot, doing odd courier work along the way. Made it four months and halfway to the Starbond Sea before we realized we'd never be able to save up enough for passage on a boat, much less a jet."

Blathnaid laughed. "Also, we wore out our shoes."

"Then we just...got older. Got fond of sleeping under roofs. Now here you are, and I know nothing about you."

Mette pursed her lips, her eyes everywhere except Orin. "I have a lot of things I want to ask you, Orin. Thousands of things I want to tell you, but it never seemed like there was any point. We should have at least tried."

Orin flushed. "We never had time and you refused to answer my questions!"

"Port!" the stagecoach driver called down to them. They stopped moving. The driver opened the door and the smell of salt immediately hit their noses.

"We can talk more on the boat," Mette said, sliding from her seat and onto the boardwalk. "The spell book I *borrowed* is one of the oldest in the library. Looks like it was brought over by the original colonists. There was a whole chapter dedicated to people like us that someone stapled into the back. It's handwritten and I know...I know, I can see the look on your faces. But it references us, Orin! Not us specifically, but this brain connection of ours. It happened a lot right after the planet was terraformed and, well, you can read about it yourself if you want. The point is that I *can* make it work, but you have to be present, and I need help with the logistics." She lowered her voice. "We could be sleeping through the night in *two days* if you'll trust me."

Sleep sounded glorious. Magic did not. Orin looked over xir shoulder at Blathnaid, who gave a lopsided grin. "In if you are. I've never been on a boat before and if you die doing this, what will I do with all the buckets we've amassed over the years?"

"Did I ask you along?" Orin asked Blathnaid as xie hopped from the doorway next to Mette, Blathnaid just behind.

"Technically, Mette did." He grinned wide enough to show most of his teeth.

Orin rolled xir eyes and turned to Mette. "I want to see that book and read the spell before you try anything. You know I just sell dandelions, right?"

"I do now. I was hoping to use your sales pitch more than your product though."

Orin blinked into the noonday sun.

"I...You know, I really thought you were going to be the princess."

Mette snorted and took Orin's hand. "Well, you dream big, don't you? I can boss you around if you want. Get on the boat. I promise you won't be disappointed."

Chapter 4

"You want to use the ceremonial flame as a glory hole?"

"Don't make it sound dirty. That's a real thing in glasswork." Mette canted her head, narrowed her eyes at Orin, and sighed. The sun beat mercilessly down on the trio as they leaned against the white railing of the jet ship, whose propulsion neither Orin nor Blathnaid understood. It went fast. That was all that mattered.

Moderate waves smacked into the sides of the ship and occasionally sprayed them, which helped wash off the stink. They had enough money for a cabin room—there was no bank on the boat to cash in Orin's note—but Blathnaid didn't think it was fair to subject other passengers to their aroma, even for a three-hour boat ride. Orin agreed. Better on the deck anyway, where no one could hear them talking about living in each other's heads.

"Glory. Hole," Orin repeated. "Listen to yourself."

"I don't know how you could have spent as much time with me as you have and not understand how to work glass. Or the names for basic glass working apparatuses."

Orin tucked a strand of wet, salty hair behind xir ear. "I don't see you growing plants."

"Farming weeds is a waste of time. At least with glass you get sellable results in a short time frame and genetics don't change every time a bee comes by." She set her jaw. "Focus. I need a bigger flame than my shop can handle and the ceremonial flame they light for coronations is perfect. It takes up most of the back plaza and they tightly control the temperatures so they can fuss with colors, which gives me the size *and* control I need to not cook you alive when you hop inside it. If Blathnaid can work the temperature mechanism and you can distract anyone trying to stop us, I can 'borrow' the raw materials and make what we need to focus the magic."

"Which is...a glass tube," Orin repeated, still trying to understand Mette's plan. "What?"

"Well, a *sleeve*. It used to be called a parchment sleeve, if we're being particular because the early versions shown in the magic book were made from thin scraped hide and set on fire. The person on the inside of the sleeve, inside with the fire, died and often the people on the outside got burned up after. That's why this one will be made of glass, so in theory, we won't die. And glass helps me control the temperature of the flame better, so Orin shouldn't die, either." Her cheeks flushed. "The early colonists didn't like having their minds fused. Everyone who set foot on the planet had it happen. No one knows why. But it's less common now, to the point of being almost eradicated. Genetic drift maybe."

"Or the plants that triggered the magic were culled during terraforming, or died off with the Dragon Droughts. The planet lost more than half its edible biomass. Which. Hmmm." Blathnaid mulled, chewing the inside of his lip, before saying, "We're not going to light Orin on fire, correct? Just use the glass sleeve to focus the magic, which involves heat from fire? Orin will be inside the sleeve with the fire?"

"Right, and it's the temperature that matters, and we can get the glass as hot as the paper, and it'll just get soft instead of combusting. This is about controlling the magic, to the degree we can. Controlling the reaction. There may be a better way to do it, but I'm not a magician. I'm a glassworker."

"I'm not either of those things," Orin said. "How do I get inside a burning hot piece of glass? Especially without burning myself. And how do you even make something like that in the middle of a palace?"

Mette's voice turned conspiratorial. "They made some potting mistakes for the coronation. Some are huge and you're pretty short, Orin. Honestly, I think we can stack three of them end to end, and then a ladder would be sufficient to get you in."

"Short? I hadn't noticed," Orin muttered and turned toward the water. Xie slipped xir hands inside the pockets of xir canvas vest. The fabric was dull and thin from years of use, but Blathnaid had lined the interior of the pockets with dragon hide. It wasn't soft but it was warm, and watertight. Inside each pocket Orin kept a crumble of dandelion seeds. They rolled so perfectly between xir fingers, never tumbling out, never slipping away. No matter where Orin went, no matter how bad the sales, there were always these seeds and a chance to start over on new soil. Well, a chance to start over if xie wasn't a human briquette.

"We don't have to do this, Orin, if you don't want to. I guess I assumed you would. The puking. The headaches. It has to stop."

The wind had torn Mette's hair from the remains of the coils, and it whipped around her face and neck in long, frazzled strands. In the direct sun, the wear to her clothes was impossible to miss, as were the old burns on her hands and arms. She was so much brighter in the flesh, so much more vivid. Orin's fingers twitched at xir sides, responding to a need Orin couldn't yet name.

"We visited each other every night. Every day. We've lived each other's lives," Orin said.

"We have. We've grown together. We've changed." Mette smoothed a wrinkle across her chest. "We've changed in many of the same ways. The laws of probability would find us unplausible."

"I can't remember my life before you. The memories are colorless and fragmented. But I remember that day in the dandelion field. I remember that night."

Mette came up beside xir and leaned over the boat railing. Their arms barely touched—a whisper of chilled skin and salty air. "That was when our lives, this life, started."

Across the froth of the sea Orin saw a mirage. It congealed from the waves and sunlight, an image halfway between fantasy and memory. Xie saw the three of them in a small house amongst a field of dandelions, the heads of the plants set to full seed. Xie could see the sun hit the white fluff and shimmer in time with Orin's heartbeat. It looked peaceful. It looked easy. But it didn't make Orin feel complete, and it came with too many questions they'd not yet answered.

"This is *magic*, Mette. Old magic. It doesn't make any sense to me. You really think you can do this without killing one of us?"

Mette placed xir hand over the top of Orin's. They'd stood this close hundreds of times in the past but never in sounds and smells and touch. Mette squeezed, her fingers curling around Orin's, and the familiar pain tickled the back of Orin's head. Xie had a flash of double vision until Mette took a step back. The mirage across the ocean brightened until Orin had to squint and look away.

"I'm tired, Orin. You're a piece of my soul but I would smother you with a pillow if I thought it would get me a full night's sleep. So no, I can't guarantee anything, but I sure would like to try."

Orin squinted against the brightness, searching the—well—delusion, for any sign that it might be a future, and not just xir brain making a pointless wish. "It's not just our lives we could lose."

"Lose?" Mette asked. "Think of how much we could gain. I'm afraid of who we will become if we don't."

The imaginary house in the dandelion field cracked apart. A wind pulled at the waves and a cloud sliced the sun, swirling the dandelion fluff and the house fragments, a cyclone of momentary fear and half-formulated desire.

"Yeah. Yes. You're right." Orin turned from the ocean, to Mette, and smiled as best as xie could. "Without the suffocation part though."

"Think how many more dande...lion ferns you could sell if you didn't look half dead all the time."

Orin playfully jabbed a finger toward Mette's sternum. "Lion ferns sell themselves, friend. I bred my own variety over half a decade. You can't find a better latex producer in the small plant area. Highly portable, hardy, a good source of vitamin C, if you're in a bind, and... Why are you staring at me?"

"Because I feel like I've never seen you before. Not like this, anyway."

Orin didn't think, because thinking just led to talking and excuses and xir—eventually—in a hot glass sleeve. Xie stepped into Mette and kissed her, barely brushing lips that tasted like ocean salt. Mette grabbed Orin by the elbows and pulled xir closer for a single heartbeat—before a wave of double vision and nausea backhanded both of them.

An explosion in a glass tube would have been kinder than the explosion inside Orin's head. An invisible hand, an invisible dragon cart, smashed into Orin's chest and drove xir back, back on xir still-soaked backside, across the deck and into the railing. The force—the magic, the whatever—held Orin there, pinned to the railing, forcing the air from xir straining lungs. It drove Mette to the other end of the deck, holding her in place against the door of their cabin, while Blathnaid yelled and scrambled between them.

In that moment without movement, while Orin's head still rang and xir heart raced, xie reveled in the softness of Mette's lips, and the taste of her tongue, and the glide of her hand, just for a second, across Orin's cheek.

"Orin!" Blathnaid had xir by the shoulders. Xie came free from the railing, pitching into Blathnaid and bringing him down onto the deck with xir. "Orin! Orin talk to me."

"Dandelion house is an impossible dream," Orin muttered. "Just heartbreak."

"I hate this," xie heard Mette say as the magic released her, and she pulled herself to her feet. "It isn't fair."

"It isn't fair," Orin repeated, like saying those words might convince the universe otherwise.

Blathnaid brushed his backside off, very clearly mulled another round of *are you okay,* before saying, "If you're both done with the worst experiment ever, you should come over here." He walked back to where they'd placed Mette's carriage cooler. On top of the cooler was Mette's stolen book: *Old Earth Magic: Tips and Tricks.* From its pages hung a red felt bookmark, which Blathnaid quickly referenced. From that section he ripped a handful of pages and held them out to Orin. "There are some side effects listed in this part I'm not too keen on."

"I had planned on retuning that," Mette said with a snort as she drew, cautiously, near.

"It already has a stapled section. What's one more? Here, Orin. You need to read this."

Orin stood and moved behind Blathnaid, putting as much space between xirself and Mette as possible.

"Memory loss," xie read out loud, following Blathnaid's finger. "Problems with equilibrium, speech, hand-eye coordination, and heart-burn." Xie blew into Blathnaid's ear. "None of this looks that bad. I just got punched across a ship for kissing."

"Ahh!" He batted the air and scooted away. "I'm trying to help you, jerk. This is all on top of potentially burning to death. Besides, you don't think memory loss is a problem? What if you forget Mette entirely? What if you forget me?"

"You'll be right there to remind me." Orin took his hand and squeezed it. "Just make me some eggs. The smell alone should bring me around."

Blathnaid stood, placed the book on his chair, and came over to the rail to the left of Mette. "You don't want to take this seriously? Fine. But here's my professional opinion: I don't know enough about magic to tell you if it will work. The book is real though. I recognize the name of the author. Fen's been giving me weekend lessons for years. He used to talk about her—the author—in hushed tones. It's a real spell. You get lowered into a hot sleeve, er, something cylindrical at a set temperature,

Mette says the words in the book and in theory, your *otherworldly connection* severs. That's specifically what this spell and the sleeve were designed to do. No one wanted to live this way if they could help it."

"We don't have a choice though," Orin said. "I..."—Xie started to say, *I wish we did. I wish anywhere during this, we'd been given a choice,* but instead said—"No, that's wrong. We do have a choice. And Mette and I are making it together."

"That's great, and I'm here to help, but have you forgotten that we have to break into the castle courtyard during the coronation to even get access to the fire, and we have to steal special coronation pots and whatever other tools Mette needs? Then we have to stack the things without being noticed, glue them up—however that is done—drop you into it without burning you to death, and then somehow get you back out once the whole incantation is done. The spell working won't be the miracle."

"We're not asking for a miracle. Just old magic to work one more time. Mette's glass can control the spell reaction. It has to, because there's no other way forward." From xir pocket Orin pulled three dandelion seeds. They sat on the tip of xir index finger, stuck there against the mild breeze and the setting sun. The three continents of their planet all lay along the equator, which made every day summer and every night, spring. On the water it was always the blistering August of Illinois in July, or so Orin remembered xir great-aunt saying once, in a distant memory. In the heat and humidity here, of the Starbond Sea, the seeds all but baked on Orin's finger, the hard hulls of xir varietal threatening to crack open at any moment.

"Seeds?" Mette asked, walking dangerously close to Orin.

Orin's senses doubled. Each wave crested twice, each seagull's cry split xir head into increasingly maddening segments as the noise reverberated from Orin, through Mette, then back to Orin again.

One of the seeds popped, hopping from Orin's finger like kettle corn, puffing into sun-kissed fluff and hovering—despite breeze and salt—in perfect parallel between Mette and Orin's eyes.

In that moment there was no nausea. No pain. The sounds of the sea, the gulls, Blathnaid's persistent questions if they were alright, all sank away. Mette's mind bled into Orin's.

They don't usually do this, Orin said, xir tone sheepish sounding even to xirself. *Usually, they just make a cute popping sound. Like a child's firecracker.*

Blathnaid's hands waved in front of Orin's face, but xie stayed, as rooted as the dandelion seed, and the plant from which it had come.

Another magic, Mette said. *One that is less important than what binds us together. Ignore it. We have a task.*

Orin snapped xir fingers. The remaining seeds fell into the ocean. Orin snatched the hovering one from the air. It came away, but burned the cold of flaming ethanol. "Gah!" Xie flung it from xir hand, toward the sea, but it clung to xir skin—a sear of impossible yellow and white heat.

"Here, give me your hand." Mette took Orin's hand by the wrist and used the other to claw at the seed now lodging into Orin's skin. Her fingertip connected to the flame, to the seed, to Orin.

The world around Orin turned to ocean. The ocean, again, turned to a vision. This time, Mette came with xir.

"It's beautiful," Mette breathed. "I see a field of dandelion fluff. I see a two-story house with a ceramic roof, like on Earth. I see us, Orin. We're in that house. We're smiling and we're happy."

Orin saw it too—the acres of yellow and white, the house so perfect it mandated a dream. Xie held xir breath, knowing what would happen when xie exhaled, or looked too closely, or started to believe in a future that didn't involve violence. *It's not real. It can't be real. I will not get attached. I almost went overboard for kissing Mette. I will* not *be seduced by magic visions.*

"Oh Orin. The house has pink shutters and lace curtains. There's a building out back I think...yes! For glass work, but hobby work. Art work. Not production. And I see a garden with gloves your size across a trowel. If I look through the window here...ah! There's at least three bedrooms. I bet Blathnaid lives here, too. Your found brother, me, and you. No buckets by the bedsides, either. What is this place,

Orin? Where are we? Are you here? Why can't I see you?"

Orin was short. Xir lung capacity rivaled that of an enraged toddler. Breath exhausted, xie closed xir eyes, exhaled.

They slid from each other in a frictionless glide. Mette fell away from Orin's mind, but no nausea followed. In a solitary breath Orin was back on the boat, back holding onto the rail, with Mette by xir side. On xir palm lay the seed, still hot but not uncomfortably so.

"It's funny," Blathnaid said, leaning in to inspect the seed. "After that last horrible idea, I expected more—"

CRRRRRRACK!

The seed blew apart with a force wholly inappropriate to its size. It sent Orin toward the ship's bow, and Mette toward the stern, tumbling and flailing, skin scraping against wood. Not magic this time but a solid exothermic reaction that nearly took Orin's hand off at the wrist.

Orin stilled—after three backward summersaults—against an iron safety rail. Mette lay dazed twenty or so feet back, her arms slung across the same rail. Blathnaid, whose face had been the closest to the seed, exhaled a mixture of curses and Orin's name.

"You okay?" Orin croaked to Mette.

"Bruised, but okay." Mette stood and came to Orin. She started to offer a hand, but thought better of it. "We never learn, do we? Distance from now on. Distance seems safer. What happened to your pants?"

Orin's pocket with the dandelion seeds had burned away, leaving a hole of charred, frayed cotton and a blister on Orin's skin. Was heat the problem? Heat and magic were related, weren't they? Xie thought Blathnaid had said so, once. Maybe. The sun was hot, overhead. But...no. Orin's pocket wasn't hot. Not magic-level hot. Which left, what? The dandelions?

"That needs aloe." Blathnaid did offer Orin a hand, which xie took. Xir leg twinged under xir full weight, and the blister burned against xir trouser leg.

"They're not exploding dandelions," xie said, prodding the blister even as Blathnaid smacked xir hand away. "I've made those, but these were just, I mean they were just seeds." Xie looked up and met the tired, sad eyes of Mette. "I'm sorry. We keep trying, and we shouldn't."

"This time was better though. The kiss bruised my ribs."

"Yeah." Orin considered. "That...is a really interesting point. This time the reaction was controlled. The seeds coated the reaction. Slowed it maybe, or tempered it. I...Blathnaid?"

"Still here," he responded. "Can't get off the boat no matter how many explosions you two make."

"I know, I just...hold on. Dandelions. It has to be about the dandelions. What had Mette said about old photos? Dandelions so thick they choked out whatever her parents had been trying to farm?" Orin rubbed at xir temples. The connection seemed obvious now, so obvious that it was ridiculous xie and Mette had never stumbled upon it themselves. "Mette?"

Mette had wedged her back against the side of the boat and was slowly sinking back to a sitting position. "What?"

"What are the chances your parents actually farmed dandelion? Strawberries bring in a lot of money. Strawberry farmers don't go bankrupt. Dandelions are a hard life. Dandelions seed and hybridize and take constant control to keep varietals intact."

Mette's eyes focused and locked onto Orin like a guided, flower-shaped missel. "I suppose that's a strong possibility, isn't it?"

Blathnaid shoved the torn pages into his pants pocket. "Makes sense. Dandelions brought you two together, and dandelions can tear you two apart. And Orin's dandelions are on their way to the coronation, where Mette's giant fire sleeve thing is also located."

"That's a lot of coincidence," Mette said.

Orin shrugged. "Our lives seem to be built on coincidence. But if dandelion was the catalyst, maybe it's the control, too."

"What are you thinking?" Mette asked.

"I don't know yet. But when you steal those pots, bring the dandelions in them, too. Toss a few in the sleeve with me maybe. It can't hurt, right? I just don't know how much to use." Xie tapped xir burned pocket. "Look what just a few seeds did?"

Mette took the book back from Blathnaid, sans ripped pages. She managed to get her feet back under herself, strapped the book back to her plastic bin and removed three glass bottles of water, offering one to both Orin and Blathnaid. "I only know my part. I'm really good at what I do, you two, and lifting a few potted weeds isn't hard. As long as Orin can keep people talking and keep selling them on not needing to check on the fire as long as xie can, I think we'll be just fine. Once we are in the courtyard we will need five minutes, tops."

"We have to *get* to the courtyard first, and our big talker, Orin, has to go in the sleeve at some point," Blathnaid pointed out. "And we have to gather enough dandelions for this to work. However much that might be. To do all this we need a big distraction. Something monumental."

Orin leaned back against the railing and slid down to xir bottom, copying Mette's previous pose. Plants. Lion fern. Heat. Not dying. Xie did a few quick calculations. Xie had sold fifteen plants to Lady Lorimette's guy. Each plant had four flowering heads. Each flowering head had a hundred or more seeds—at least Orin's variety. Three seeds had almost blown xir and Mette's heads off but before that, they had stabilized their connection. How much did Mette need to stabilize the exothermic reactions of magic? That had to be the trick to staying alive. The colonists had severed their connection, but the separation had been violent, hot, and killed at least one party. If they could stabilize it...coat the reaction like one might coat a live wire in rubber, maybe the kickback wouldn't be so bad.

But how many dandelions did it take to shore up wild magic? If the seeds were going to absorb heat, Mette would need a lot of them. Maybe all of them. None of Lady Lorimette's dandelions had gone to seed yet, either, which meant tossing in yellow plants and turning them directly into fluffy white flumes. There'd be no controlling that reaction, not once it started.

"I've got an idea," xie said, groaning. "But it's really sticky, and I don't think either of you are going to like it. And it's definitely going to put me out of business."

Chapter 5

People called Methalimus a castle only because stone had been used in its construction, Orin was certain. No part of it looked at all like what children's stories described. The walls were bare cinderblock with occasional red brick façade. Oval-shaped and somehow coming to a triangular point, the parts that could be considered roof were covered in wood shingles. The courtyard sat on the west side of the building, and its dividing wall was just a square of river stones stacked only a bit higher than Orin's head.

Sitting poorly on the stone wall were Orin's dandelions, all now repotted in round bottles of various sizes from Mette's factory, which explained why the man who'd bought them looked so familiar. They were custom pieces, Mette had informed xie, and they had gone back and forth on design for several months. The final plans hadn't been clear, and the glassworkers had made the pots in every size originally listed, which made for a very eclectic collection. The lion ferns were uniformly in full bloom, which swelled Orin with enough pride that xie could almost forget about the whole sleeve thing, and the burning to death thing, and kissing Mette, and the upcoming incineration of a lifetime of horticultural study. Almost.

"Did I engineer this varietal because of hard work and science, or because of magic?" Orin asked no one in particular.

Blathnaid slapped xir back. "As long as you don't talk to dandelions in your head and they talk back, I don't think it matters. Stay focused."

"You sure you're not just, oh I don't know, jealous of my innate magic?" Orin elbowed Blathnaid in the ribs. "Eh?"

"Ow, you're pointy, and no. I've worked my entire life to get access to six spells and you urinated on a dandelion at six and got magically bound to a decently"—he made air quotes with his fingers and Orin snorted— "attractive woman. You also have to blow up all your work to separate from her. At the end, in End, I still have six spells."

"And I might get that 'decently' attractive woman."

Blathnaid shrugged. "Seems like a fair swap either way." He poked one of Orin's dandelions. A nearby guard scowled, so Blathnaid poked the stem again for good measure. "Where is said attractive woman who isn't your soul mate because that position is filled, thank you very much?"

"Right there." Orin pointed to Mette, currently power walking through the crowds of coronation shoppers. Dawn had only just broken—the air burned with a distinct chill— but coronations of potentates happened only every ten years. Stalls were open. Souvenirs and snacks abounded. Guards yawned and futzed with their communication devices, completely unconcerned about the early morning revelry.

"Sorry it took so long," Mette said as she ran up next to Blathnaid and Orin. She held two round loaves of bread and three thin glass jars of juice in her hands, and handed them out. The sun only just peeked over the stone rooftops of the city of Methalimus, and the breeze smelled like wine and pollen. White plumeria flowers hung across every doorway, their yellow insides a gentle compliment to Orin's blooming dandelions, which littered the palace walls.

Orin ripped xir bread in half and offered one side to Mette, who politely shook her head and stepped back the moment Orin's hand looked like it might brush her own. "Had mine in the shop. I couldn't carry three along with the drinks."

"We appreciate both." Blathnaid took a long swig from the bottle, finished it, and placed the empty glass in a padded, cylindrical bin marked GLASS REC. "As well as the lodging and the showers."

Orin grunted in assent as xie chewed a too-big bite of potato bread. The shower had been glorious, as had been the faces of every one of the factory workers they'd had to walk past to get to them—Mette quelling questions with her glare as she led them through. Orin had offered to spend the blank note on lodging for the night, but Blathnaid had argued that there were a dozen or so better uses for the money, and Mette had offered her room at the factory.

So, the three had all ended up huddling on the floor on a pile of blankets because no one could agree on who should take the bed and...

They'd slept through the entire night.

They hadn't been touching. Mette and Orin had Blathnaid wedged between them, and for the first time in forever, Orin awoke only with the morning sunlight.

And...oh, everything just *smelled* different when you got to sleep through the night. The world seemed to have more color. Mette, too, seemed different—her eyes bright as she stumbled awake, still drunk on a solid night's sleep. The morning had seemed so full of possibilities, in that moment of waking. No need for burning glass and crashed coronations. They could just all travel together, work together, *be* together....

Except. They could travel together and work together, but they would never be able to even hold hands in friendship, not without the headaches and the puking. And if Orin forgot again, and some evening the twilight twinkled just right, and the breeze was still, and they were drawn together...

"You're not having second thoughts, are you?" Mette asked, bringing Orin back to the present. "Or are the clothes too tight? You want a thick, tightly woven wool for this, trust me. I know it looks like a jumpsuit, but you don't want your clothing catching fire."

Orin did not now, nor had xie ever, given a damn about clothing. An unfortunate protrusion in xir chest made some shirts fit tighter, but a slit up the side quickly relieved the issue. Here, now, there were much bigger matters at play. "You slept last night, didn't you?"

Mette's smile fell away. "Yes. The whole night. You too?"

"Yes. I..." Orin scrambled for words as Blathnaid struck up a conversation with their nearest guard over the cost of juice. "I didn't expect this," xie said at last. "This draw between us. I should have. It's silly that I didn't. We've been pulled together since we were children. Of course, meeting in person, it would be that much stronger."

"Spending every night close enough to touch you, and not being able to, wasn't really the solution I was looking for though."

Orin felt heat rise in xir face, saw the same mirrored on Mette's.

"We need to do this," Orin said.

Mette nodded. "I know."

"I don't have any seeds on me anymore. We slept through the night. Maybe, I mean. We could try. Science demands replication."

"So does manufacturing." Mette stepped into Orin, her breath a waft of fruit juice and flowers. "One more try."

Orin's fingertips traced Mette's jawline— both sets of skin weatherworn and calloused. They tangled into one another, Mette's hair a knot of silk against Orin's palms, Mette's lips a wholly different kind of fire on Orin's neck. Nausea rose and Orin internally screamed *No! Stay down. Stay away. I will have this moment. And then a thousand moments like it afterward. This magic does not control me!*

"Uhh, Orin?" Blathnaid called from somewhere off to xir left. "I don't think that's a good idea. Take a look at this."

Xie pulled Mette up and in, standing on xir tiptoes to reach full, juice-stained lips.

"Orin seriously. You need to look at your dandelions."

They both waited, an eighth of an inch apart, sharing each other's oxygen. Orin's stomach rolled but xir breakfast stayed down. *What if. What if last night had been the key? What if the seeds on the ship had been the key? What if it was already over? What if they kissed here, now, at the edge of the Gated City, and the only thing that happened was that their tongues danced, and that Orin found Mette's waist, and the opening to her shirt, and then maybe a quiet inn just outside the city....*

Orin closed xir eyes and brushed xir lips against Mette's, like the dance of a paintbrush on silk.

"Orin *stop!*"

Blathnaid pulled xir away just as pressure built on Orin's chest. The smell of juice mingled with the taste of bile. The sun blinded Orin momentarily as Blathnaid spun xir around and pushed xir forward, into the wall, xir face pressed against one of Mette's glass pots.

"Bfwanid," Orin said. "Stopf."

"*Look!*" Blathnaid released xir, brought the pot down, and held it right in front of Orin's face. Orin had sold the dandelions in clumps of four. They'd been separated to make more pots, leaving just two per container. The pot in front of Orin had a solitary dandelion, its yellow petals dripping into white fuzz. The other flower, the twin, lay shriveled and desiccated, wound around the survivor like a noose.

"When I kissed Mette?" Orin choked out. Xir skin still sparked from Mette's touch, and Mette's breath, and the promise of their teased future.

"The moment you got within a handspan of one another. Look." He pointed down the wall, where a dozen other pots showed progressive stages of death and seeding. Guards argued, loudly, over the plants, completely ignoring the trio.

"I hate this!"

"So fix it." He put the pot back on the wall. "Why are you fighting something you've wanted your whole life?"

"Because..." Orin's words faltered. Because Mette's hair was buttercream, and her skin a calloused tapestry. Because Blathnaid was an amazing friend and Orin wanted that *and* whatever Mette was. Whatever Mette could be. Because there was a puzzle here that involved seeds, and heat, and magic, and if there was more time, they could solve it. Time, and resources, and money, and...all the things none of them had ever had.

"I...so...the three partial sleeves?" Orin asked when xie couldn't think of what else to say. There were no words to describe the death of a dream so freshly born that it had never had a chance to be vocalized. Xie wiped xir lips on the wool sleeve of Mette's gifted jumpsuit. "I can draw crowds away, and will have to draw them far enough that the dandelion combustion won't affect Mette and I, but can you—Mette, and Blathnaid—move the large pots you need on your own?"

"I've got a hand cart." Mette's eyes stayed on Orin's lips. Her hands balled to fists, knuckles raking along the waist of her pants as she crushed down her own emotions. Then she let out a long exhale that Orin could almost feel. "As long as it doesn't tip, we're fine. What about you? Got your distraction thought through? It's magic we're playing with. It's unpredictable. And it's cruel."

"Magic isn't sentient." Blathnaid took Orin's hand' and squeezed it. "It's neither cruel nor kind. Neither is life. We both know that." He raised his free hand up, fingers splayed. Tiny yellow sparks danced across his palm. "Magic's never done a whole lot for me either, despite how much I chase it. But I'll help out, however I can."

Orin picked up the glass-potted dandelion nearest them off the west side of the wall. The living flower stretched for xir, straining the soil. Xie touched the dead one instead and through xir mind flashed an impression of Mette, tangled in her nightgown and bedsheets, unmoving and huddled on her bedroom floor. The only way out was through, it seemed. Very literally, through a glass tube.

Orin held the pot as far away from xirself as xie could and said, with very little conviction, "I've got it under control."

* * *

Lady Lorimette rode an impressively large grey Komodo dragon and *wow* did she look imposing, riding without saddle or harness. She was regal, in starched and ironed orange cotton pants and a bright yellow linen shirt. Her hair shone a deep russet in the sun and her skin was so dark it reflected blue highlights. She rode alone as tradition demanded, but thousands lined the sidewalks on either side of the brick and cheered or booed, depending— Orin surmised—on their political affiliation. Some of the children beat handmade drums, and in between the cheering, Orin caught snippets of normal, everyday conversation. The weather. The economy. Magic—a relevant topic, as Orin counted at least two hundred people with Blathnaid's green in their hair. The wind had turned mild, the clouds dispersed, although smoke from the ceremonial flames dulled the brightness of the sky. The air smelled of smoke, but it would be another hour or so before the princess walked through the ceremonial flame. The staff in charge would wait to fan it to its hottest point until right before she appeared in the courtyard.

"Time!" Blathnaid whispered into xir ear.

Orin ran.

Xie dodged around children and pets and almost lost an ankle to a dwarf Komodo someone hadn't thought to leash properly before breaking out of the crowd and into the main parade route. The dragon made another lunge for xir ankle at the same time, and Orin tripped, landing on xir knees on the brick, pot carefully cradled in the crook of xir arm. The living dandelion reached for xir cheek and stroked it like one might a pet rabbit. Nausea rolled Orin's stomach but xie did not budge.

The princess's dragon reared. The startled Lady Lorimette lost her grip and slid backward off its body and onto the street. The dragon—exceptionally well bred—settled immediately. Lady Lorimette did not.

"Get out of the street!" she hissed. Orin heard running feet on brick. Likely the guards—who had been half dozing at their posts—approaching.

With the dragon stilled, Orin opened xir eyes as wide as xie could and walked forward on xir knees, potted dandelion held out in offering. Xie'd removed the dead one—well, Blathnaid had removed the dead one—and the year-old, giant survivor spun wildly in the breeze, drawn to Orin, drawn to the sun, drawn to whatever magic made up the planet at large. Magic's mark seemed more prevalent here in Methalimus. Blathnaid's green was an outlier in End, to the point where he occasionally dyed his hair. In the main city it seemed downright fashionable.

The almost-queen/potentate scowled in the bright sunlight, and Orin caught the faintest green tinge to her eyelashes. Xie reevaluated xir plan, mashed in what xie now knew about dandelions, straightened, stood, and offered Lady Lorimette xir widest, most enthusiastic smile. "I'm with the royal gardener and Lady, you forgot your flower! You can't forget *this* flower." Xie leaned in, xir voice conspiratorial. "You know about the recent advances in dandelion research, right? It's the unifying factor you've been waiting for. Think of the *message*."

Guards shouted and pleaded with the crowd to part.

"I...But I wasn't supposed to carry one during the procession, I didn't think." Lady Lorimette batted at the leaves that Orin thrust into her face. "What research? Who are you?"

"Why, about the magic of dandelions!" Scattered gasping came from those nearest them. Orin tried to push the pot on Lady Lorimette again as she swung a leg over the dragon's back, attempting to remount. When she still didn't take it, Orin pulled a silver badge from xir pocket with xir picture, license number, and description of xir business etched into the face.

Xie turned xir smile to a disappointed frown. "I came all the way up from End this morning to make sure the dandelions your man bought from me were ready to release. This one in particular—when you carry it in— it will bloom the moment you cross the threshold."

"But that's not magic, is it?" Still the lady strained to get a clear shot of Orin's face. Orin, being not much taller than a wild-grown dandelion, expertly avoided. "Aren't they bred that way?"

"Well, yes, but it's the symbolism you want, is it not?" Orin put xir free hand on xir hip. "The Head Gardener told me you wanted to make a statement. This is that statement. Dandelions are a symbol of this planet, and Earth. It blends them together. The...the green of the leaves symbolizes the magic that crept into humanity itself. The yellow is, um, you know...because both planets had yellow suns. It's symbolism, and magic. It brings magic into your governance. It'll help people in the outlying places, like End, better understand how we've embraced magic, unlike Earth which, um, is probably still burning people for it. They did that, you know. A long time ago." Xie wiggled the silver badge. "I know all of this because I'm the breeder. Here's my badge. Only the *best* breeders get badges. And my partner is a magician. He has green hair." Xie tapped xir business name, which currently read *Saucy Sequins and Prophylactics*. "We've already filed for a name change due to the, uh, um, the scientific advances. Our new name is *Daring Dandelions, LLC*. Taming historic magic for everyday needs."

Orin needed to remember that name. Rebranding with magic might reawaken the dandelion market. Blathnaid's sideshow magic would be a great selling feature.

One of the guards finally managed to break out, and a heavy hand fell on Orin's shoulder. The dandelion slipped forward in xir arm, and xie didn't have to manufacture xir look of panic. Xie kept xir badge out.

"Lady!" Orin and the guard said at the same time. It had only been about two minutes. Blathnaid and Mette needed at least one more before Orin joined them. Xie just needed to make this sale. This one last sale.

Lady Lorimette paused mid-mount and scrutinized the silver.

"You didn't read any of your letters this morning did you, Lady?" Orin asked. Stocky fingers bit into xir shoulder as the guard awaited instructions. The crowd sounded either closer, or louder. Orin caught snippets of conversation. Xie heard the word "magic," whispered like a curse, and then by another person, whispered like a joy. Panic grew on Lady Lorimette's face as well, which helped steady Orin's nerves. A little.

"No. There was too much to do and...I...must have forgotten." Lady Lorimette shooed the guard. "Let the gardener go. Xie's right." The Lady's shoulders squared, and she addressed the crowd. "Magic belongs here. You belong here." Her eyelashes fluttered, comically, but also clearly for effect. "We all bear the mark of this planet. Physical manifestations do not indicate worth. Let the dandelion, which grows on both of humanity's worlds, which binds us to our ancestors and to this planet, be our guide and our symbol. That which is pulled, and crushed, poisoned and incinerated, but always returns. This is us. This is humanity that sailed into the stars and colonized a wild, vegetative world with untamed magic and made it their own. We are, my people, the dandelion!"

Cheers erupted and the teeming mass of humanity screamed Lady Lorimette's name.

Orin jerked free of the guard and thrust the pot into the lady's hands. Something scaly brushed xir calf. Damn dragons and people not following leash laws. "Don't forget this!"

Lady Lorimette took the pot and held it above her head. "The dandelion!"

"The dandelion!" the crowd chanted. "The dandelion! The dandelion! We are the dandelion!"

"Lady?" Another guard finally emerged from the crowd, taser drawn. "Your 'gardener' is delaying the procession. We should continue on."

Almost. It was *almost* time. Just a bit longer.

"THE DANDELION!" screamed the crowd.

Lady Lorimette remounted her dragon, the pot cradled in the crook of her left arm. "I can't believe you all let me forget about the dandelion delivery and the symbolism. I almost missed this opportunity if the gardener hadn't pressed in. Get your hands off of xir. Go back to your posts. You're disrupting the procession. You're disrupting *me*."

The first guard whistled and both bowed but couldn't make as hasty a retreat as they'd hoped. As Orin planned, the crowd had spilled onto the street, eager to see the figurehead dandelion. Orin turned to see two dozen guards stuck amongst at least four thousand people. They tried to herd the crowd but even with whistles and taser threatening, the crowd wasn't easy to move.

"DANDELION! DANDELION!"

"Am I clear to carry on?" Lady Lorimette asked Orin. "What else should I know for coronation, since my people couldn't be bothered to give me instructions?"

Orin had to get right up to the lady's ear in order to be heard. Xie managed it by getting a knee up on the dragon's shoulder, xir other foot dangling precariously in the air. "This plant is my own unique cultivar. Licensed and patented. The seeds are showy *and* have healing properties. All natural. You place it on the throne when you get in and stay really still for at least five minutes while I snake a little acetylene torch around the back and flame it until it goes to seed."

"That's the magic part?"

"No." Orin tried to get closer, but xir knee slipped and xie had to grab what xie thought was the dragon's ear in order to stay upright. "They're a magic *symbol*. They do magic stuff but that isn't important. You just need a metaphor for the yellow turning to white seed. Like...humanity spreading with adversity or something." Orin's pocket buzzed. Mette was ready. "You'd better go. They're looking for you at the castle."

Lady Lorimette's attention turned to the castle's oval door, only a hundred or so feet away. A head edged from the left side opening, and a panicked face assessed both the crowd and Lorimette's chances of making it through without her dragon clipping someone at the knees. 'Frothing' would not have been an inappropriate word for the current crowd state.

"You are dismissed then. The guards can clear a path." She clapped her hands and the two guards that still glowered at Orin, turned their attention to their future potentate. "Where are your colleagues? I need through this crowd and to my castle. Now."

Her dragon snapped its mouth in agreement. The guards unclipped the batons from their belts, ignored Orin entirely, and began to wedge a path through the crowd. The guards in the crowd surfed toward them, slowed by the exponentially increasing bodies.

Orin jumped once into the air, startling the woman behind her enough that xie could slip behind her. Xie dodged back into the thick of the crowd, a tiny human missile running as quickly as xie could to the back courtyard entrance, the fire, and Mette.

Chapter 6

"Psssst!" Orin located the sound and looked up as xie ran along the courtyard wall. Blathnaid leaned over the stone between several glass pots, gesturing for xir to come closer. Three guards lay unconscious in the street. Orin didn't ask questions.

"Door just a few meters down. It's unlocked. The rest of the guards are all dealing with the crowd. Nice work."

Orin coughed in the thick smoke. Visibility was limited this close to the courtyard fire, but Blathnaid already had the side door open. Orin ran in. Once inside, oppressive heat joined the smoke. The ceremonial fire spread out in a ring about ten meters in diameter—blue at the base and orange at the tips—and was constrained by a ring of grey cinderblocks. An array of glass-working gadgets cluttered the ground. Blathnaid stood at what looked like a control panel, adjusting knobs and frowning. Scattered around the courtyard were Orin's dandelions, dumped from their glass vases but still well alive in their mounded dirt.

Towering from the middle of the flame was a red-orange glass tube. It was twice Orin's height and maybe three times xir width. The glass was thick and green in the places where it was cooling, but red hot in others. The glue lines were both easy to see, and sturdy looking. At least Orin wouldn't be crushed to death.

"You're late," Mette said as she tossed a thick pair of gloves onto the brick. No emotion in her words, but Orin didn't blame her. They'd already made this choice. There was no reason to dwell. "It's almost too cool to work. Hop in. I'll get the incantation started. How many of those"—she pointed to the dandelions—"do you want to take in with you? Or should we throw them all in after? They weren't part of the original spell, so this is guesswork."

Orin stared at the glass monstrosity. The heat felt like it might raise welts if xie got much closer, and the opening was well above Orin's head. "I don't know how many dandelions. All of them? And how do I get in? Did we bring a ladder?"

"Got it!" Blathnaid stepped away from the controls and shook a wooden ladder from flat to tripod just in front of the sleeve. His face, already sweating, turned cherry red. "Don't cook in there, okay? I'm not going to raise your dandelion seeds if you die. You have to live, if only for them."

"You're about to BBQ me with my dandelions," Orin muttered. The fire was hotter than xie'd imagined. Beyond scalding. Beyond burning. The ladder would catch fire if left against the sleeve much longer, what with the ceremonial flames licking at its legs. Xie needed all the control, all the buffering, xie could get. Louder, to Mette, Orin said, "Toss them all in. After I'm in. We shouldn't risk you handing them to me. Not when we're this close and time limited."

"Hey! You can't be in here! Come out now." The voices came from the other side of the wall, but Blathnaid had barred the door. Still, the wall was easily scalable, although the smoke made it hard to see. They had negative time.

"Now!" Blathnaid yelled. "I'll toss in the dandelions. Just get inside!"

Mette opened the book and started to read a string of nonsense words. Orin ran to the ladder—the wood already darkening—scaled to the top, hands blistering from the heat, and stopped. What...what did a life without Mette look like? What did a life *with* Mette look like? What price were they both about to pay?

"Orin!" Blathnaid yelled.

Orin's vision doubled. The back of xir skull pounded. Xie saw through Mette's eyes as she sank to her knees in pain, still reading from the magic book.

"The plants ready?" Orin asked Blathnaid.

"Got them all!" he called back up.

That was that, then.

Blisters popped on xir hands. The soles of xir shoes became sticky. Tears flooded xir eyes and Orin jumped without looking, off the top of the ladder and into the center of the glass cylinder.

Xie landed on the hard ground, scraping already torn skin and crying out from a jammed elbow. There were spurts of fire inside, but matchstick amounts. It didn't matter. The air, the ground, all melted along with Orin. Outside, Mette insistently read words in a language xie barely understood. Dandelions rained upon xir, clumps of soil hardening in the heat, yellow flowers bursting to ribbons of white seed pods as they floated down, or up, as the wind allowed. Orin moved to xir knees, biting into xir tongue, and refusing to scream. Xie focused on the sky instead, on the long, thin packs of seeds that floated on the air currents, landed, and stuck, semi-permanently, to anything in their path. They'd have been hell to see through for the coronation ceremony and were likely hell on the guards and grounds crew now, as they tried to scale the wall and choked on smoke and seeds. Mostly they stuck to Orin's burned skin. They clogged up xir nostrils, choked xir mouth, wedged into the corners of xir eyes. Orin could see, yes, but only through Mette. Xie could see the spell book, hear the guards shouting, hear the chanting of DANDELION! from the coronation crowd. Xie smelled smoke and burning flesh, and underneath that, the subtle perfume of the flower that had ensnared Orin and Mette's lives.

"That's all of them!" Blathnaid's voice sounded as sticky as Orin felt.

Orin's skin started to bubble. Xie heard part of the door to the courtyard break apart. "They're in!" Blathnaid's voice choked. "Hurry up! You two need to hurry up *please!*"

"...*officinale!*" Mette screamed the last word and slammed down the cover of the magic book.

The world extinguished.

Chapter 7

For a moment, there was no light and no sound. Just pain. Blisters searing open. Tears that evaporated before they could form. Dandelion fluff danced across burned skin, the sensation like millions of tiny, ice-covered needles piercing Orin's flesh.

Then, like a curtain being pulled, the rest of the world flooded back in. Where there had been only orange-red, however, now the glass was thick green and cool. The ground around xir was white with fluff, the seeds as thick as marshmallow. Orin's clothes had burned away, entire portions of xir skin had burned away. Xie wept clear fluid across substantial parts of xir body while dirt and seed clung to others.

Sweet air blew into the sleeve, settling some of the blisters. Cooling xir skin. The dandelion seeds did not stir, remaining a bed upon which Orin fell back, exhausted.

"Orin?" Blathnaid's voice came, muffled, through the glass.

Xie still heard the guards—blustering and busy—scolding Mette and Blathnaid, complaining about the coronation and the plants, trying to hurry them out and relight the flame before Lady Lorimette proceeded. No more laying around. Orin had to move, no matter how much it hurt. Xie flexed xir forearm and popped the blisters that marred the skin. More of that clear fluid dripped onto the ground and Orin clenched xir teeth and eyes against what felt like a hundred Komodo dragons, all driving their teeth in at the same moment. An acid bath would have been more comfortable.

Xie breathed deeply, trying to get past the pain, and startled in the perfumed smell of dandelion. No longer an undercurrent, it swept inside the sleeve. It pushed away the smell of human sweat and crisp human skin. In that moment, Orin smelled xir childhood, and the dandelions xie and Blathnaid had harvested for dinners when their money ran out. Xie smelled their first small garden, where Orin had perfected dandelion breeding at ten years old. Xie smelled the End market and the dandelions that finally brought in enough money to pay rent.

Xie smelled the farm Mette had been conceived on. Or at least, what that farm should have smelled like.

Wind caught in the tube, creating a small cyclone. Orin looked up, eyes watering against the dryness, to watch a snow of dandelion seeds loop from the ground, to the opening of the tube, and back down again. They blanketed xir skin and clothes—a rain of soundless cotton candy fluff. On the exposed skin, blisters cooled and deflated with seed contact. The seeds formed a patchwork film over the open wounds, closing them to the air. Orin stopped shaking, not knowing when xie'd begun. The cyclone settled as quickly as it'd begun. Again, the world stilled. This time it had far less pain.

Had they controlled it then, the heat? The magic? Or were the dandelions themselves the magic? Did it matter?

"Orin?" Blathnaid tapped on the sleeve, panic in his words. Xie saw his deformed outline through the glass, looking more mushroom than person. "Orin! Answer me."

"Alive," xie croaked back. "Guards?"

"From what we can see, Lady Lorimette is in hysterics about the flowers going off before her arrival. Her dragon is the only thing out there that *isn't* panicking. The crowd is either delighted or terrified, and I can't tell which. There's dancing in the streets, but we've got people on the ground holding their heads, too. You don't think...no. I don't want to think about that. Anyway, a few guards broke in but left when the dandelions went off. Can you get up?"

Orin managed to stand—a human clothed entirely in white dandelion fluff. There was also...not disorientation really, but...clarity? Xir vision had definitely sharpened, and this time it wasn't due to sleep. Xie hadn't realized how many crisp edges the world had or how quiet the air was, even with all the yelling.

"I don't think I can climb out. Ladder?"

"Sure thing. Hang on." Orin saw Mette's silhouette turn and walk away, and realized, abruptly, what was going on. Orin saw only what was right in front of xir. Xie hadn't realized how much of Mette seeped into the corners of xir vision, and how much background noise came from Mette's own ears. And now, *now*...wow. Just *wow*.

They had done it.

Still Orin waited, unmoving. Xie heard guards and yelling, Blathnaid cursing and Mette shouting that they needed to go. Orin stood in an island of fluff and searched for sadness, a sense of loss over this woman xie barely knew but who had shared xir mind for years, but felt...what? Hope? Joy? Maybe ...anticipation?

Even after the ladder came cascading down, nearly decapitating xir in the process, even after xie climbed out of the glass tube and Mette caught xir eyes, even then, there was no double vision. No headache. No nausea. There was just Orin. Just Mette. The pull between them, the pull that Orin hadn't realized existed, had broken apart in the glass tube and now there was...what?

"Well?" Blathnaid asked after Orin jumped from the top of the tube and landed hard on the ground. He pulled Orin into a hug before Orin's hiss of pain backed him off.

"It's done."

"And you're alive. You're also naked, kind of."

The words seemed callous, but Orin heard the relief in them, saw Mette's hesitant approach. Xie held out xir left hand and Mette took it, and there was only air between them, and dandelion, and fragments of obsolete lives. Now there was only Mette—tired, stained, shadow-eyed Mette. They could have anything they wanted now. Well, almost anything. This time, as Orin ran xie finger over Mette's knuckles, no image of dandelion fields played in xir head. No futures with adorable houses populated xir vision. Xie saw Mette. Only Mette.

"You okay?" Mette asked. "It...isn't what I thought." Their hands remained tight together, Orin lifting up Mette's hand to kiss those knuckles, but felt nothing afterward. Mette didn't step any closer. She licked her lips, dry from the fire, but this time, Orin didn't move in. They were strangers now, passing acquaintances at best.

"Yes. You?"

Mette nodded.

"The people outside?" Orin asked. "Was the cost more than us?"

Mette shrugged, her eyes never leaving Orin's. "If we reinvigorated some old magic, let them find their own way out. Maybe this time it will be a priority for the government. Maybe this time people will be believed. We paid our price, Orin. We get to be done."

"I agree. I suppose they could make their own ceremonial flames. It's a strange tradition. Maybe that's where it came from—to separate the original colonists." Xie shrugged. "If we can figure it out, they can too." There really wasn't anything else to say. Orin searched for words to fill in the silence, but Mette shook her head. Orin understood.

Something that looked like fireworks went off in the corner of Orin's vision. The coronation had to continue, of course, even with a problematic, maybe magicked crowd. It bought them a few moments more. Xie stared at Mette for another breath before taking Blathnaid's hand and motioning toward the port. It did no good to keep staring. "We're going to cash that note before this scene settles, and they realize what happened. I don't think we're going to go back to End. I'll write, sometime. Tell you where we are if you want to visit. If you want. No pressure."

"Maybe." Mette sighed. "Orin, do you think...?"

Orin gave her hand a final squeeze, then released it. "We made the right choice. We can make another one, later, if we want, but right now, this"—xie pointed at the glass—"this was good."

Mette smiled sadly. "Yes. Yes, I know." She leaned in and pressed her lips briefly to Orin's. No magic beat at their bodies. No visions overtook their minds. No spark leapt from Mette's lips. Orin kissed Mette the way she might kiss Blathnaid—quickly, briefly, affectionately but without passion.

Mette said, "I'm glad I don't have to smother you with a pillow. Take care of yourself, Orin."

"You, too." Orin smirked, then whispered into her ear. "Princess."

Mette grinned as Orin and Blathnaid turned and walked back through the gate and into the crowded street. There would be time to be sad, and time to celebrate. But for the first time ever, Orin could see a future. It involved sleeping through the night without pots by xir bed, it involved a full-time job where xie didn't have to worry about passing out. It involved travel. Eggs for breakfast. Friends. Adventure. Xir own mind. Xir own space.

And eventually, maybe, once xie and Blathnaid landed on xir feet and figured out who they were, that future might involve Mette. Surely, with enough time, they could find each other again. There might be a mess to clean up, too, if their dandelion explosion had bound up the people of Methalimus. But this was their break. They'd paid the cost a thousand times over.

Now, now it was time to live. Now, it was time for some really excellent naps.

ACKNOWLEDGEMENTS

This novella began its life as a 12K short in a nonbinary anthology. Issues with one of the anthology authors lead to the book being shelved, which gave me the opportunity to expand the story to where I'd always wanted it to be.

If you're new, welcome to a silly story about dandelion latex (a real thing!), dragons, and bittersweet love.

If you read this story before, prepare for about 10K more of emotions, dandelions, and magical worldbuilding. This time the world gets to breathe, although Orin, unfortunately, does a lot more puking.

ABOUT THE AUTHOR

J.S. Fields (@Galactoglucoman) is a scientist who has perhaps spent too much time around organic solvents. They enjoy roller derby, woodturning, making chainmail by hand, and cultivating fungi in the backs of minivans. You can find their books at jsfieldsbooks.com and support their writing (as well as get exclusive short stories, Ardulum snippets, and sneak peaks at new works) at http://www.patreon.com/jsfields.

Please take a moment to review this book at your favorite retailer's website, Goodreads, or simply tell your friends!

Made in the USA
Middletown, DE
28 April 2023